To Joe — A FAC

Rodney Paul

10/6

Baggy Zero Four

A Forward Air Controller in Vietnam

©Rocky Raab

This book may be ordered from the publisher

The P.R. Department, LLC
479 Hiland Rd
Ogden, UT 84404
USA

Or through the printer at www.lulu.com

Preface

This book is completely fictional. Any resemblance to people, places or events is purely coincidental.

The war in Vietnam, however, was all too real. Like all wars, it brutalized participants and innocents alike. It can be said that everyone involved, on both sides and in whatever regard, came away as victims – but also as victors.

Nearly 4,000 pilots served as Forward Air Controllers in Vietnam from about 1965 until 1973. They conducted combat missions in light aircraft over heavily defended areas in Vietnam, Cambodia and Laos. More than 200 of them were killed or went missing in action. Only one FAC captured alive by the enemy was ever released or heard of again. Most FACs were recently commissioned, fresh out of college and flight school. No other imaginable flying job could heap upon them more responsibility, more danger or more futility than being a combat FAC.

The events in this book are an attempt to describe but a thin slice of the incredibly diverse world of the Vietnam FAC. For further insight into the real world of FACs, the reader is invited to explore the website of The FAC Association at www.fac-assoc.org.

Rocky Raab

Baggy Zero Four

CHAPTER ONE

It was as if the world had farted in his face. The air that came in through the jetliner's door hit him like garbage gelatin: smothering hot, with overtones of sewage, dead fish, diesel smoke and jet exhaust. It was Cam Rahn Bay, Republic of Vietnam, and First Lieutenant "Rusty" Naille knew his nose would never forget that first olfactory assault as long as he lived. How long that might be was up for grabs.

"Jesus H Christ, what *is* that?" He asked, staggering back a half step and bumping into the Army sergeant behind him.

"Just 'Nam, sir," the sergeant answered laconically. "You won't get used to it."

Rusty was too overwhelmed by the stench, heat and humidity to look at the man, and he stumped down the rickety boarding stairs. The flight attendant's face at the bottom featured a completely plastic smile as he whisked past. But she could afford to be disingenuous: she was leaving within the hour. Rusty and the other hundred and fifty soldiers who reluctantly staggered from the jetliner's cool interior would be here for a whole year. At least the lucky ones would. Some would go home broken, mangled, burned or emasculated. Others would go home in ominous aluminum boxes, and still others would never go home at all. The question on every mind was: which group was he in?

Rusty (his birth certificate and official Air Force records mutely listed him as Virgil Anthony Naille) was a Forward Air Controller or FAC. His job would be one of the most demanding, awesome and awful, not to mention riskiest, that a young man not long out of college could attempt.

The job of a FAC is to fly low and slow over enemy territory, seeking out lucrative targets or protecting allies on the ground. He'd control airstrikes, artillery and perhaps even naval gunfire, serving as air traffic controller, diplomat, quarterback, translator, radio relay and reporter – simultaneously. And while he did all that, he'd be flying his own tiny propeller-driven plane, navigating from obsolete and erroneous maps, avoiding midair collisions with lumbering helicopters and supersonic fighter-bombers, furiously writing cryptic notes in grease pencil on his cockpit windows – and getting shot at.

Rusty staggered - cramped and stiff from the 22-hour flight - into the Cam Rahn Bay Passenger Terminal. As he waited to present his orders and ID card, he was shocked to see an ancient Vietnamese woman simply squat down and pee on the concrete floor not ten feet from him. What few teeth she had were ebony black, and she bared them at him in what could have passed either for an imbecilic grin or a predatory smirk. Only a few of his fellow passengers even cast a glance. None of the clerks or guards seemed to notice, and neither did any of the other Vietnamese scuttling about like larger versions of the black and white flies that infested this hangar.

Rusty stared numbly at the back of the departing old dame until a finger poked him from behind.

"Sir? Hey sir! Unit?" The sweating clerk at the table in front of him repeated, head cocked and dripping eyebrows arched in exasperation.

"Huh? Oh. Uh, 21st TASS. I'm a FAC," Rusty added, lamely.

"Uh huh." The clerk smacked Rusty's orders with a date and time stamp, spraying them with perspiration from his hand. "Can't help you, sir. But there's a phone over there," he said, not looking up again, or even gesturing to where "over there" might be.

Rusty took back his stamped orders and wandered over to where a huge pile of identical duffle bags had been unceremoniously dumped off the back of a truck. His was in there somewhere. When he finally found it, most of the other arriving soldiers had been herded

2

into groups by Army sergeants with clipboards. There were no Air Force people in sight, so he shouldered his bag and started looking for a phone. Down a corridor, he finally found an occupied office and a bored clerk who dialed the 21st Tactical Air Support Squadron for him.

An enlisted clerk answered, "21st TASS. Airman Schmidt. This line is not secure."

"Hi. I'm Lieutenant Naille. Uh, reporting." He said, dully, mind still reeling from the combined impact of jet lag and the stultifying air.

"Oh, yes sir! Welcome to sunny Vietnam! We're expecting you. You at the portal of doom?"

"Um, you mean the Passenger Terminal? Yeah. I mean yes, airman. How do I report to your headquarters?"

"Oh, no need for that today, sir. You were only expected yesterday. Tomorrow will be soon enough to report in. Just hitch a ride from where you are up to Tent City. See ya then."

See ya then? Rusty stared at the now-dead phone. What kind of laxity was it that a lowly airman could banter like that with an officer? It was impertinent, maybe even punishable. Anger struggled briefly to arise within the fog of his numbed brain, but lost. Rusty shambled out into the glaring sun and palpably humid heat. A jeep slid to a dusty stop nearby.

"Hey newbie! You need a ride?" The jeep's driver was another Air Force officer, a captain in camouflage fatigues, grinning at Rusty.

"Uh, yeah, I guess so…sir."

"You can drop the 'Sir" shit. We's all just plain ol' niggers here, boss," the man said in a poor and tastelessly fake dialect. "Where you headed?" He jerked his thumb to the back, indicating where Rusty could heave his duffel.

Rusty stared dumbly for a heartbeat, then blurted, "Tent City I guess."

"Malaria Manor? Oh brother. You really are an FNG, ain't ya?"

"FNG?"

"Fucking New Guy. How long you been in 'Nam?" The captain squinted sideways at Rusty as he popped the clutch and roared away up the hill.

Rusty grabbed convulsively at the seat edge – there was no door - and said, "I guess maybe an hour."

"An hour? *One hour?* Oh, my bleeding ass. A Vietnam virgin! Jesus fucking Christ, if I had three hundred sixty-four days and twenty-three hours of Viet fucking Nam ahead of me, I'd cut my own fucking throat!" He skidded to a stop and nodded towards a line of tents. "But maybe by morning, you won't need to." He drove off cackling madly to himself.

Rusty stood looking dumbly – again – at the back of a departing person whose behavior had been so disconcerting as to stun Rusty into immobility. Finally, he coughed from the dust and turned around. Ahead of him stood rows and rows of what looked to have once been white canvas tents, but which were now a strange pinkish orange. They seemed to be not just unoccupied but abandoned. Too tired to explore either the rationale or the layout, he stumbled down a path between two rows, passing perhaps ten tents before he simply turned and entered one at random.

Inside, the heat was even more stifling. A dozen empty iron cots each held a rolled mattress, a pair of folded sheets and an olive-drab wool blanket. Rusty unrolled the mattress on one, set the sheets aside and dropped his duffel bag nearby. Stripping off his already sodden uniform, Rusty flopped onto the stained mattress. Before he could even marvel at where he was, or think about his wife Mary Beth, he was asleep.

He woke to a pervasive whining sound and the feeling of being stung by nettles. To his horror, he was covered with a writhing gray fuzz of mosquitoes. With a cry of primeval alarm, Rusty slapped and wiped off mosquitoes until his skin was red with the blood they had already sucked from him. On the verge of panic, he swept up the heavy wool blanket and wrapped himself in it, leaving only a tiny hole to breathe through. Inside it, he could feel a few of the pernicious pests still biting, but he couldn't slap at them without uncovering areas of skin which were instantly attacked by even more of the whining horrors. He lay bathed in increasing floods of sweat, alternatively dozing and waking in the agony of fierce itching until the clouds of mosquitoes miraculously disappeared. It was now pitch black in the tent and Rusty tossed off the bloody and sweat-soaked blanket in favor of one of the sheets, which he wound tightly about himself in the event of further attacks. He tossed and turned despite his deadly fatigue, frantically scratching himself, sweating and starting up at every new sound.

When the tent began to show a faint hint of gray light, he rolled groaning from the cot. His bladder was bursting, he had clotted blood all over his body, and he itched so bad he thought he might scream. The only thing on his mind was how to find a shower and a toilet. Rusty staggered out of the tent, following the wooden duckboard path until he came to a corrugated fiberglass structure that had to be the toilet. It was, and after he voided his bladder, Rusty found that the other side of the divided facility was a shower. The water was cold, and Rusty now shivered under it, but it ran dark red across the floor as it washed away the remains of the pestilential feast. Somehow, it also reduced the fierce itching.

Great, thought Rusty. If this is an indication of what Vietnam is like, I may join the stupid hippie protesters when I get home.

By the time he felt halfway human again the sun was fully up. Emerging from the shower, Rusty stopped, looked all around and realized he had no idea which one was his tent. He walked down one set of duckboards, peeking into each tent he passed. Some seemed in use but vacant, others were bare, and a few had cots but no residents. He shook his head in consternation when he realized all the occupied tents had mosquito nets over the cots. None of the tents looked like

5

his. He retraced his steps and tried another direction from the showers. Nothing again. The third time, he managed to see his duffel bag and the now-bloody mattress through the open flap. His duffel had been emptied and ransacked.

Rusty donned a mix mash of uniform bits, stuffed what little remained back into the duffel and found his way back to the dirt track he came in on. Within moments another jeep careened to a stop.

"Holy shit, man. What the fuck happened to you?" the Air Force sergeant driving it blurted. "Man, you look like you got mumps, measles and maybe even leprosy. Fuck me." He laughed.

"Uh, what? Do I look bad? There wasn't a mirror in the head. And my stuff got ransacked, so my uniforms…"

"Oh, fuck the uniform. Nobody gives a rat's ass about that. But man, you got *eaten* in that joint! You'll be lucky if you don't come down with the screamin' meemies."

Still groggy and disoriented, Rusty suddenly realized he was being addressed by a sergeant. "Sergeant, do you always address officers in that way?"

"Fuck yeah. Hell, *lieutenant*, over here, I probably outrank you. Damn sure I'm more important around here than some grab-ass college snot. What are you, a supply weenie or somethin'?"

"No, I'm a FAC."

"A FAC? No shit? Oh well then. That's a different bowl of weed. Yessir, that's a whole 'nuther thing. That rates a 'sir' all right – 'specially with the grunts. You hop in here, Lieutenant FAC, sir. I'll take ya wherever ya need to be." He looked hard at him as Rusty tossed his much lighter duffel bag in the back of the jeep. "You're a FAC for real? No shit?"

"Yes, why?"

"'Cause FACS usually look like they have their shit together. But you look like you just been mugged by every whore on Tu Do Street. No offense."

Rusty almost managed a smile.

The 21st Tactical Air Support Squadron was a tin hangar down on the flightline. But it was air-conditioned, and the blast of frosty air that belched out of the door when Rusty entered felt good on his madly itching skin.

A clerk was typing furiously, and started talking before he looked up, "Morning. Who would you like to…Christ! Uh, I mean…umm…Sir, is there something wrong with you? Do you feel OK? Why don't you sit down and I'll get you a wet cloth or something."

"Yeah, that might feel good. But I'll get it. Which way is the head?"

The clerk motioned down the hall, and watched open mouthed as Rusty turned that way. In the latrine, Rusty jumped back at the sight of himself in the mirror. His face was red-splotched, swollen and puffy with bites. His eyes were bloodshot and had crusty yellow gobs at each corner. Even his ears were swollen. His sandy blonde hair stuck out at all angles and he had clearly needed a shave about two days ago. He splashed water on his face, smoothed his hair back with his fingers and shrugged. The rest was beyond repair.

Back at the clerk's desk, a Major now stood. He flashed a bemused grin at Rusty. "Damn. Fleming here said you looked like a bag of three-day-old dog shit, but he always exaggerates. Or at least he always had until now. My God, what happened to you, Naille?"

"I'm not sure, sir. I landed yesterday and somebody here told me to bunk for the night in Tent City. I did, but the mosquitoes were awful, and then my duffel got ransacked, so I have almost no uniforms left – and no shaving gear," Rusty rambled.

"Fleming, do they have a medal for most fucked up arrival in-country? If they do, put this Lieutenant in for one."

"Don't think so, Major. You want me to try for a Purple Heart? He sure did bleed as the result of hostile action with enemy – um...what's that word? Oh yeah! Collaborators." The clerk grinned up at his boss.

"You know, that actually might fly." He turned from the clerk to Rusty. "But the question is: can you fly? That's what I need to find out. And I will. But not today. You'll need a few days to get resupplied with gear, and some more time for that swelling to go down."

"Yessir," Rusty said. "Um, isn't there paperwork and such to be done now? I need to report in."

"Hell, you just did. Nah, Fleming here will fill all the I's and cross the boxes and dot the T's. This is Vietnam, Naille. Nothing here goes the way it's supposed to."

Rusty pulled aside his parachutes harness and shoulder belt restraints, then pointed to the sewn logo on his breast pocket. "We are talking the United States Air Force, right? The one that has now trained me to fly for a total of eighteen months, the last six months of them specifically about how to be a FAC?"

"Yes, yes," said Major Spring, "Of course. But that was in the US. This is Vietnam."

"So I somehow forgot how to fly when I crossed the International Date Line? I see. And now you have to teach me how to do *this*." Rusty deliberately jerked the control yoke of the Cessna O-2 roughly about, sending the tiny twin-engine craft into wild gyrations.

"Oops! Stop that! Now!" The major clutched at the edge of the protruding glare shield over the instrument panel until Rusty stopped. "No, that's not it. I'm just seeing how you rate as a pilot. It has to do with where you'll be sent now that you're in-country."

"But Fleming tells me pilots are assigned as the need arises: a position opens and the next available new guy gets sent there."

"Well, yes. That's true. Uh, I mean, it is kind of true. Not always, though. It varies."

"What varies is that Academy grads get the plum jobs, while ROTC or OTS guys get shithole assignments. Isn't that right?" Rusty glowered at the major. He'd seen the huge Air Force Academy ring on the major's hand. Knuckle knockers, that's what they were called by non-academy officers, men and women who'd gotten their commissions after four years of Reserve Officer Training Corps studies on college campus; or who'd come up from the enlisted ranks via Officer Training School. The knuckle knockers – or "zoomies" - were the Air Force's good old boys, and zoomies looked out for each other at every step.

"Oh, no. That never enters into it," the major blithely assured Rusty, waving his hand dismissively though the air.

"Then it's purely a coincidence that the last two zoomies to arrive here got assigned to Vung Tau, while every ROTC grad in the last month has been sent to god-awful Army camps, right? Zoomies get Vung Tau? The Vietnamese Riviera?"

Rusty had been given a room in officer quarters, and had talked long and late into the night with several other newly reporting FACS, some who'd been at Cam Rahn for several weeks already. While all awaited in-country assignment, the 21st TASS put them through "FAC U" which supposedly was graduate school for being a Forward Air Controller, but which seemed to all of them just a square-filling exercise: make-work of a kind. While his grotesque facial swelling had healed, Rusty had little to do but sit in the lounge and bullshit. He'd learned that the knuckle knocker network was alive and well here. Hell, it thrived everywhere there was more than one blue-suiter, apparently. Knuckle knockers came in, flew a few orientation flights and were immediately assigned to working FAC units – invariably to cushy, safe and high-profile units where there was an excellent chance to win career-enhancing combat medals.

Those who'd gotten their commissions other ways (harder ways, some thought, given the anti-war and anti-military riots on many college campuses) seemed to get assigned only after much delay and many unneeded "remedial" training flights like the one Rusty was flying now. And when they DID get assignments, they were shuffled off to one of the remote scrapes in the red clay known as Landing Zones. The Army owned those LZs, and Army brass was not known for overexertion in nominating non-Army officers for medals.

"Um, well, FACs do rotate out of places like Vung Tau, you know. They have to be replaced, too." Spring asserted, but coloring a bit in obvious mendacity.

"Sure. It just happens that zoomies get those assignments and ROTC guys just happen to always get places like LZ Buttwipe. Purely coincidence," Rusty said, mimicking the major's insouciant hand flip perfectly. "We'll just see who goes where for the next few weeks."

Except that Rusty didn't get a chance to do that. Spring rated him as combat ready immediately after that flight. The very next day he was assigned (ahead of three other guys who'd been at FAC U longer) to the Army outpost at LZ Emerald.

Gee, imagine that, he thought to himself.

CHAPTER TWO

Seen from a small cargo plane, the only green thing about LZ Emerald was the jungle that surrounded its barbed wire perimeter. The Army apparently hates vegetation or anything else living, Rusty mused. The place was one huge and ugly red scar in the earth. They bounced down on the rough dirt runway, dodging two oblivious UH-1 "Huey" helicopters who crossed their path on final approach. Out of his circular window, Rusty saw hundreds of troop tents aligned in rigid rows, a few clapboard-sided buildings with tin roofs here and there and a rickety control tower standing amid a score of aircraft protective revetments.

Everything that stood above ground was surrounded by waist-high walls of sandbags, and whatever looked like it might be mostly below ground was roofed by mounded sandbags. And absolutely everything was permeated through and through by red clay dust. The predominant color of every fixed thing in sight was pinkish orange.

If I'm here to keep this idiot country from turning Commie, it's too late, Rusty thought. The cursed place was already red.

Out of a cloud of yet more red dust, a jeep was approaching. It squealed to a stop, and Rusty waved to the driver: another young Air Force pilot in a flight suit.

"You the new guy?" the driver asked.

Rusty nodded. "Yup. Rusty Naille. You?"

"I'm Bob Strunk. Rusty Naille? You shitting me? That your real name?"

Rusty pointed to his embroidered nametag and shrugged, smiling. "Well, Naille is real. I've been called Rusty most of my life. It was sort of a joke in grade school and it ticked me off a little at first; but even my parents eventually started using it. I kinda like it now."

"Cool. Let's get you up to the hooch and bunked in. You'll meet the rest of the gang, or most of 'em. Nice bunch, mostly. The place sucks, of course," Strunk said as he popped the clutch and roared off.

"What's it like?"

"Oh, it's a complete disaster. All the charm of a ghetto but without the sophisticated population. The world's anal orifice. Should I go on?"

Rusty laughed, despite the depressingly clear visual proof of what Bob had described all around him. "Kind of a shock after Hurlburt."

"Oh God, don't remind me about Hurlburt...sugar sand beaches, soft Gulf breeze in the pines, brick quarters with air conditioning, hot and cold running maid service, television. Geez, Rusty, why'd you have to bring all that back to mind? Not to mention the easy flight schedule. Oh, Lord. That was heaven."

"Yeah, I loved FAC school. I might move back there when this is all over. You could do worse than living in the Florida panhandle."

"Yeah, that's for damn sure. Worse as in here, for example. Couldn't get much worse than this hole. Not just the location, either."

Rusty groaned to himself. There had to be a people problem. Or a mission problem, which would be no better. Dreading what he might hear, he asked, "So what about the job? What's it like FACing here?"

"Oh, that's actually not so bad. We do all the usual FAC stuff, visual reconnaissance, intel gathering, running air strikes and stuff. We also support some long-range patrol teams. That can turn out to be the proverbial hours of boredom or else the moments of sheer terror. Both, on some days. The official mission is to support the Army brigade. Their idea of "support" seems to be for us to jerk their asses out of the fire with air strikes without getting credit for it, and

12

take the blame when they try to do things themselves and the effluent hits the rotating airfoil. Well, here we are: the FAC Shack!"

Strunk gestured grandly to an ugly, decrepit shack built of plywood with a corrugated tin roof. A row of 55-gallon steel drums surrounded the lower walls, with sandbags stacked atop those almost to the building's low eaves. Rusty had thought it was a condemned hut until the jeep stopped in front of it.

"Home sweet hovel, Rusty. Be sure to wipe your boots on the way out so you don't get the world dirty."

Bob gestured proudly at a small porch-like affair that was screened in. "That's our party zone. The only screened porch on the whole LZ. AND the only private hot water shower, too," he said, pointing now to a galvanized garbage can standing precariously atop one corner of the porch.

Rusty wondered about the garbage can as shower but was too morbidly curious about the rest of the hovel to ask for an explanation. They passed through the porch and stood just inside an interior door. The single room inside was lighted by a pair of flickering fluorescent tubes, and featured three pairs of bunk beds arranged around the other three walls. All were draped with mosquito netting tacked up from ceiling to floor.

"I guess you may as well take that one right there," Bob said, indicating the lower bunk on his right. Unless you really want an upper," he said, looking at Rusty with one raised eyebrow.

"No, I'd rather be in a lower. But why wouldn't I want an upper?"

"Rockets and mortars, of course. The lowers are behind the shrapnel walls, and it would take a direct hit inside to get you. But the uppers are vulnerable to a hit anywhere nearby. Crazy Eddie actually likes to defy the gods, as he says. He sleeps up in that one. See the bare wood behind his bunk? A rocket hit right outside that spot on top of the sandbags one night. It took most of the roof off, and wrecked that wall. Turned the mattress on that bunk into a sieve, too. Crazy Eddie says that's now the safest spot here. Kinda like the 'lightning never strikes twice' argument, I guess. But that's just Crazy Eddie. The rest of us sleep on the lowers."

"Thanks for telling me. I'll tell you a story about lightning some other time, but right now, how many of us are there living here?"

"Lightning story, huh? I can't wait. Anyway, four of us live here: me, of course, and Crazy Eddie and Brian Bigelow. Plus you. Eddie is Ed Palmer, but nobody ever calls him anything but Crazy Eddie. You'll see why," Strunk said, laughing to himself.

"Brian is acting as stand-in Ops officer up in the TOC and Crazy Eddie is up on a mission. The two other Air Force officers assigned here are Major Whitworth and Captain Blake. The Major is our Air Liaison Officer and Blake is his Operations Officer. Both of them have offices in the Tactical Ops Center and they have quarters up with the senior Army muckety-mucks. Blake is an okay guy to work for. He's off somewhere at a meeting today, which is why Brian is standing in for him; but you'll meet him tomorrow. Major Whitworth is okay too, but something of a cold fish. Only uses last names – stuff like that. And then we have four crew chiefs to maintain our three planes. They live in a tent down near the flightline. But enough about us. What about you?"

"Well, I'm new in country. This is my first assignment. I'm from downstate Illinois and went to St Louis University. English major. What else is there to know?"

"Oh, tons of stuff, Rusty. But that'll all come in time, I guess. Number one important fact: you a drinking man?"

Rusty laughed silently. "Yeah, I have been known to tipple. Not a lot; I'm no lush. But I do enjoy a martini or a beer at night."

"Martinis, huh? Boy, you'll be a genuine fair-haired boy with the Colonel. That's Colonel Ardmore, the brigade commander. He's a weird duck, a Napoleon. He's a colonel in a brigadier's slot and it pisses him off that commanding this brigade hasn't gotten him his

14

star. So he struts around like a peacock with a cocklebur up his ass and is insanely jealous of anyone higher up in his command chain. One example: he learned that a one-star at another brigade holds formal mess every evening, so Ardmore feels like he has to go one better. He holds a mandatory all-officers cocktail hour followed by a formal mess every evening. And the martini is his official drink dujour. But you'll see that, too. Soon, in fact. You have a clean uniform? If so, get unpacked and change into it. The Ardmore Hour is almost upon us! Oh joy of joys," he said, rolling his eyes.

Bob left while Rusty emptied his duffel bag into the empty locker at the foot of his bunk and then changed into a set of the new fatigues he'd gotten as replacements at Cam Rahn Bay. He momentarily groused once again at having his uniforms, travel kit and photos of Mary Beth all stolen that first night in Malaria Manor. And that made him look at the double layer of mosquito netting around his bunk, partially in dread that it might be needed and partially in relief that it was there. Just as he finished dressing, he heard voices approaching.

"Hi there, bud! You must be Rusty. I'm Brian."

Walking in with Bob was another First Lieutenant of medium height and weight, brown hair and deep blue eyes. He sported a trim reddish mustache on a face with several old acne pocks. Oddly, one of his ears jutted out perpendicularly from his head while the other laid normally back. He smiled and offered his hand to Rusty. "Glad to have you aboard. Want a beer?"

"Glad to meet ya, Brian. Don't mind if I do. But isn't there some official cocktail party or something in just a little while?"

"Sure is, but that's a whole fifteen minutes from now. Plenty of time to wash down the dust and prepare the gullet for juniper juice. Bob, open three brewskis while I change, willya?"

Strunk nodded and went straight to a mini-fridge out on the porch. He came back with three cold cans and handed one to Rusty.

"Carling Black Label? Oh man, I haven't seen a can of that in years! Where the heck did that come from?"

"We think it comes from some merchant marine ship that apparently left port sometime in the middle of World War II with a full cargo of the stuff. But it was so slow that by the time it got to Europe, the war was over. The Army being what it is, they sent it directly to Korea. By the time it got <u>there</u>, of course, it was too late again, so they re-routed it back to Europe to help with the Cold War. When it arrived, somebody realized that bringing Carling Black Label to Germany was too great a cultural insult even for the Army, so they just left it tied up at the dock without unloading it. Until now. So it finally got shipped to 'Nam and we end up drinking 25 year-old weasel piss," Brian concluded, tapping cans with Rusty.

"Vintage stuff," gagged Rusty after his first sip. "Man that's…uh, something."

The three of them laughed together.

While Brian changed, Bob and Rusty adjourned to chairs on the porch. "What about you, Bob? I somehow forgot to ask anything about you."

"No sweat. You had too many more important things to ask about. I'm just your average guy: born in Ohio and just stayed there. Went to Ohio State, married my high school sweetheart. ROTC and then flight training at Craig AFB in Alabama. All the usual FAC schools and then here: nothing remarkable."

"A Buckeye, huh? You an Ag major?"

"No, electrical engineering, actually. Ohio State's a helluva good engineering school – especially for a place that once elected a cow as Homecoming Queen."

Rusty guffawed and spit some of his beer. "WHAT! A *cow*? Are you kidding me?"

"No, really," Bob said, grinning as wide as his face would allow. "An almost unanimous vote for one Maudine Ormsby, who turned out after the election to be a dairy cow. She was dutifully crowned at the homecoming football game despite not actually being enrolled as a student. She declined to attend the dance, however."

Rusty laughed aloud again. When he recovered, he asked, "You play football?"

"Oh Lord no. I wasn't nearly big enough or fast enough for the likes of Woody Hayes, no matter how hard I was willing to work. Character and effort might be important to Woody, but I don't think he'll ever play a guy who couldn't help us beat Michigan." Bob winked at Rusty. "How about you?"

"Nah. St Louis U doesn't have a football team, and I absolutely detest basketball. Besides, who'd want to go through life being known as a Billiken?"

"A what?"

"Billiken. The school's team name and mascot. Imaginary mascot, I should say. Nobody could ever tell me what the heck a Billiken is or is supposed to be. The drawings of him just show a pudgy, ghostly-looking thing like a raw dinner roll. Imaginary, like the basketball team's success story."

"Ooh, that's brutal. You don't exactly sound like a fanatic alumni, Rusty."

"That's because I'm not. The only reason I went to college at all was to get into ROTC and then flight school. St Louis U was close enough for me to commute every day and it had an ROTC program. Plus, they accepted me. Those were the only three factors in picking my school. But I don't care if I never hear of the place again."

"Well, I suppose it's an opinion. Hey, we better get a move on. Brian, you decent yet?"

"Never. But am I ready for the colonel's soiree? Yup." Brian emerged from the hooch just as a jeep rolled to a stop at the door and a striking FAC jumped out. Painfully thin and over six feet tall, the most astounding thing about him was his hair. It was coal black and it stood out in a fuzzy halo a good six inches in all directions. On a black man, it would have been a gigantic Afro, but this was no Negro. This man's skin was stark white. Corpse white.

"Hey Crazy Eddie, you better go to afterburner! You'll miss the Ardmore Hour if you don't hustle. Oh, this here is the FNG, the one and only Rusty Naille. See ya on the patio!" Bob shouted over his shoulder as the three ambled off.

Rusty stared back at that incredible hair until Brian grabbed his elbow. "You'll get to see all you want of Eddie later, believe me. Let's get moving. You have lots of people to meet."

They climbed a short path bordered by rocks painted white. It rose as straight as a surveyor's line to an arc of split rail fencing. As they climbed, Rusty was able to see first heads and then uniforms of Army officers milling about on what he finally saw was a cobble-stone courtyard perhaps ten meters on a side. It adjoined the back of a building with a painted banner "Officer's Mess" along the eaves. Holding court in the curved apex of the fence was an Army bird colonel. Bob's description had been apt. The man stood perhaps five feet seven, had slicked-back, oily black hair, a face reddened from brutally close shaving and a pair of piggish, hard, black eyes above a beak of a nose that might have been stolen from Charles DeGaulle: Napoleon in Vietnam, indeed.

Before either Bob or Brian could say anything, another man walked up to Rusty with hand extended. "Lt Naille? Welcome to LZ Emerald. I'm your ALO, Frank Whitworth. We'll talk more over dinner. But first, you should meet the Colonel." As he guided Rusty towards the demi-god, the major grabbed a glass of clear liquid and ice from a tray carried by an enlisted Army man. "Hope you can stand gin," Whitworth hissed from the corner of his mouth. "Pretend you can for a sip or two with the Colonel, anyway."

"No problem, sir," Rusty managed to say just as the two stopped in front of the man. Rusty was amused to note that Whitworth seemed to stretch himself upwards as they walked – and he was about six feet tall to start with. Now seemingly even taller, he coughed softly.

The Army colonel craned his neck back, a fleeting but clear look of extreme annoyance passing over those dark features for an instant, then he said, "Yes, Major." There was a distinct note of deprecation in that second word.

Colonel Ardmore, may I present our newest FAC? This is Lieutenant Naille. He's fresh from Cam Rahn and will be ready to go to work very soon. His records show he's a promising young addition to our force."

The colonel nodded curtly in Rusty's general direction, but kept his eyes on Whitworth. "Very good. I hope he's valuable to the Army." This time, there was positive emphasis on the last word.

You really are an arrogant bastard, Rusty thought to himself.

Just then, the arrogant bastard turned at last to look at Rusty. He raised a glass of cut crystal to Rusty, whose own was of cheap, thick glass, Rusty noted. With eyes and voice even colder than the gin, the colonel said, "Cheers."

"Cheers, sir," Rusty replied, wondering if he would someday remember it as the most ironic and wildly inaccurate prophesy he'd ever heard. It was harsh gin, too.

Inside the mess hall, there were long tables and benches along a central aisle with a head table and chairs at one end. All the tables had white tablecloths, and silverware and starched napkins were arranged formally throughout. The five Air Force officers sat at the last table in the rear, and Whitworth sat deliberately with his back to the head table. He motioned Rusty to sit beside him, the other three opposite.

"Now then, Naille, fill us all in on your details," Whitworth said.

"Well, I've already traded details with Bob and Brian, but I haven't formally met Cra...I mean Lt Palmer," Rusty caught himself and extended his hand across the ironed linen.

Palmer himself laughed. "Oh, it's just Crazy Eddie. Don't worry, I'm well known as an oddball." He contorted his face into a hideous grimace and panted slightly from the corner of his mouth. It was a patently silly face, and Rusty laughed aloud, drawing disapproving stares from the nearby tables of sullen Army officers.

"Oops," Rusty said to Whitworth, "Sorry, sir, I didn't mean to create a disturbance."

Whitworth shook his head at Crazy Eddie, rolling his eyes at the same time. Then, to Rusty, "Don't worry Naille, we Air Force officers would be like red-headed step children in this mess no matter how well behaved we might act."

Rusty heard two Army officers immediately behind them snort in disapproval at that.

There followed a spate of formal toasts – several to the Army but none to the Air Force – that smothered any further talk for a few minutes. While the meal was being served, everyone got better acquainted. Rusty told his story to Whitworth and Crazy Eddie, and then Crazy Eddie filled in Rusty about himself: still single, graduate of some practically unknown school in Washington State, but more impressively, Eddie was a mustang. That is, he'd first enlisted in the Air Force (to avoid the draft right after college) and while serving as an enlisted man, had applied for and was accepted to Officer Training School. There, he passed the flight physical and went to flight training immediately after he received his commission.

"I think they found me just too weird to be an enlisted man," he joked, "and thought that since I'd surely flunk out of OTS, they'd be rid of me forever. Ha! Fooled 'em!"

"Yeah, but now we're stuck with you, and you *are* a weird SOB," Bob said, digging Crazy Eddie in the ribs with his elbow. "I already told Rusty here about you and the rocket bunk."

"Lightning never strikes twice, you know," Crazy Eddie said, shaking a stick-like finger under Bob's nose.

"Ah, but that's the turd in your punchbowl, Eddie. It does. I know. I've been hit twice."

There was sudden silence as all four men stared at Rusty. Then Brian said, "Oh that's good. Nice joke, Rusty. You had him stopped dead there for a minute."

"If it had been a joke, thanks. But it wasn't. I *have* been hit by lightning, twice. Well, twice on the ground and once more in the air while I was in flight school."

More stares. Then Bob turned to Crazy Eddie, "I think maybe you are about to be dethroned as King of Weird among us Baggy FACs."

Rusty interjected, "Baggy? That's our call sign? Baggy?" He looked appraisingly at the others, then down at his own belly. "All of us as thin as mongrel dogs. Naturally, we are Baggies. It figures."

"Sure does. This is 'Nam, ya know."

In the morning, Rusty awoke and tried to roll out of his bunk, only to become entangled in the diaphanous folds of mosquito netting. His struggles woke the rest of them.

"Christ, Rusty, you that eager to get flying? Calm down or you'll have the ceiling down on us all."

"Just have to pee is all," Rusty said. "And I may do that right here if I can't get untangled right quick."

Brian swiped the light switch from inside his own netting, and the fluorescents buzzed into flickering life. "Oh well, it's almost six anyway. We should have been up already if we don't want to miss breakfast. Here, Rusty, let me help." He ducked under his netting and unwound the folds from Rusty's head and arms. "Ok, you're free. You know where the head is?"

"Actually, no. Couldn't find one last night. That's why I'm so desperate right now. Where is it?"

"I'll lead the way. C'mon."

They followed the rock-bordered path in another direction where it forked off from the Officer's Mess. In about a hundred yards, they came to a wooden structure composed of plywood sides, a tilted tin roof and door openings at either end of its 15-ft length. When Brian shined his flashlight inside, Rusty confirmed what his nose had already told him: it was an outhouse. This one was more than just an outhouse, however. It was a four-holer. Four oval holes adorned the length of the single bench.

"Uh, you guys actually use this thing? I mean *together*?"

"Huh? Oh yeah. Real cozy all taking a dump together." He noted the look on Rusty's face. "No, it's not that bad. You'll be uptight about it at first. We all were, but not for long. You want me to stand outside for now? Until you finish?"

"Uh, yeah, I kinda do. But I think you're probably dancing from foot to foot as much as I am, so forget it. Come on and we'll water the flowers together. Maybe for a dump, though..."

"Yup, I copy. No sweat. But we aren't the only ones who use this. You might be in here solo and have an Army puke saunter right in on ya. Just be warned."

"Uh huh. Consider the warning applied."

They stood together, grinning like monkeys, and peed into the openings. In accordance with standard male protocol, neither
22

responded to the impulse to check out the other's "equipment," staring straight ahead the whole time.

"You know," said Brian as they walked back to the hooch, "you'll have a flight today with Captain Blake. Don't think of it as a check ride or anything, 'cuz it's not. But on the other hand, it IS your main chance to prove yourself. He's the Ops Officer, and if he doesn't think you're shit on a stick, you won't get many flights except boring crap like VR and parts runs."

"I copy that. I'm not worried. But what kind of guy is he?"

"Well, he's a straight-up guy for the most part. Meaning he won't stab you in the back. If you try to dazzle him with bullshit, though, he'll see right through it. In which case your ass is grass. So just be yourself. He believes in the Rule of the Wart."

"The who?"

"Rule of the Wart. You know…lots of people have warts, and having a wart is no big deal. But if you run down the street yelling 'I have a wart…' then there's a problem."

"Ahh, I see. Okay."

Captain Blake turned out to be a slightly rotund, slightly short, very Jewish man with an easy humor and a ready smile. Ironically, his head of short black hair included a bald spot exactly the size and position of a yarmulke. Rusty liked him immediately.

After exchanging pleasantries, they both donned parachutes, helmets and pre-outfitted survival vests; then tucked water bottles, maps, radio frequency sheets, lead pencils, grease pencils, sunglasses and gloves into the pockets of their Nomex flight suits. Finally, they loaded and slid Smith & Wesson .38 revolvers into underarm holsters. Thus burdened, they were ready for a couple of hours' worth of flight over the hostile and enemy-controlled territories that surrounded LZ Emerald, Republic of South Vietnam.

Rusty, in the left or command pilot's seat, ran through the detailed checklists that insured no possible detail had been overlooked. He did so by running his finger down each and every plastic-laminated page strapped to his right thigh, even though he'd long ago memorized them. Captain Blake dutifully acknowledged each and every step, even though he'd memorized them even longer ago.

When the engines were running, and the intercom turned on, Blake said, "All right, so much for the book. Now forget all that crap and let's get this pig into the sky." He dialed in the frequency of LZ Emerald's primitive control tower and said 'Baggy Zero Four, takeoff.'"

"Baggy Zero Four, roger. Taxi 31, winds two niner zero at ten, altimeter three zero zero one."

"By the way, Rusty, that's your callsign. I'm Baggy Zero Two. Whitworth is Zero One, and so forth."

"My own callsign? Cool. Never had one before."

"Yeah, I know. But over here we don't base the callsign on the mission and/or takeoff time. You get your own no matter what kind of mission you fly or when," Blake said. "Now taxi to the dogbone at the end of the runway and do your run-up checks," Blake said.

Rusty nodded, and carefully eased out of the corrugated steel revetment that surrounded the plane on three sides – protection from most rocket and mortar attacks, provided the explosive shells landed anywhere but in front of the open enclosure. He noted that the sergeant who'd helped him pre-flight the plane now jumped into a jeep and followed them. "Why is that sergeant following us in the jeep?"

"Well, he's the arming crew as well as our crew chief. He'll pull our rocket arming pins once we get in the dogbone and aren't pointing back towards the camp."

"Ahh. That makes sense. Not enough troops to have dedicated runway arming crews, huh?" Rusty said.

"Hell, they also assemble rockets, arm the planes, fuel the planes and scrounge parts besides being maintenance troops and crew chiefs. Those four do the work of six or seven different troops...each," said Blake. Then, scrunching around to look at Rusty eye to eye, he added, "And don't you ever forget it. Without them, you are a cipher, a tit on a boar hog. Copy?"

"Well, yeah, but I do fly the thing, you know."

"Fly what? The plane that THEY get ready? With the parts that THEY acquire and install? And equipped with the rockets that THEY assemble? Burning fuel that THEY pump? You may be the gladiator, my boy, but they are the ones who provide you with the arms, the armor and everything else you use to fight. In other words, you may be the spear point - they are the shaft and arm. Got it?"

Rusty was silent for a few seconds. Then, "You know, I do get it. The driver may get the roses and cold milk at Indy, but all he does is turn the steering wheel. The pit crew makes all *five* wheels work."

"By God, you DO get it. There's hope for you yet, son. If only all lieutenants grasped the facts of life that quickly, this would be a better man's Air Force."

The run-up of the engines, radio checks, propeller checks, and all sundry checklist items went smoothly, and then Blake signaled the sergeant to arm the rocket pods under each wing. As the man did so, the two pilots held their hands up in plain sight, a guarantee that neither would touch any switch or control while the sergeant was anywhere near the explosive rockets.

Once cleared for takeoff, Blake said, "You ever taken off from a dirt field before?"

"Uh, no," Rusty admitted. "What's different about it?"

"Not much, really; at least when it's dry. But because of the dust, you should run up the rear engine first, then release the brakes, and only <u>then</u> run the front engine to full power. Believe me, it helps with visibility."

"Ah ha! I'd have never thought of that. Good plan." He did so, and danced on the rudder pedals to steer around the potholes and bumps.

"Good, very good. You needn't miss all of them, you know. Too much swerving reduces the acceleration, and this field's short enough as it is."

Rusty had just discovered that for himself. The end of the field rushed towards them much faster than he liked, and their plane gathered speed with the deliberation of an octogenarian putting on his socks. He was glancing with increasing alarm between the airspeed indicator and the line of low bushes and shrubs at the end of the runway, when Rusty felt the nosewheel extend a bit: almost enough lift to fly. He eased the yoke back and checked their speed – 85 knots – and the plane gave the little sideways lurch and skitter that it always did as it lifted off. They were airborne.

The O-2 was a hastily purchased interim aircraft, rushed into Air Force service to take up the slack between the rapidly aging (and rapidly being shot down) O-1 Birddog aircraft around which the FAC mission had been designed, and the purpose-built turboprop OV-10 Bronco that supposedly would make FACs almost invulnerable once again. Except that the Bronco's introduction kept getting delayed…and delayed…and delayed. Finally, the Air Force threw up its corporate hands and bought several hundred Cessna Skymaster aircraft and outfitted them as war birds.

The O-2 that resulted boasted the fore-and-aft engine, twin tail boom arrangement of the Skymaster. That configuration allegedly made for easier transition training from single-engine planes, added multi-engine reliability and boosted both cargo capacity and range. Allegedly. It might have done, had not it been for the added weight of a huge radio pallet that replaced the rear seats, two rocket pods and the associated wiring slung under each wing, added fuel tanks with fire-suppressant foam filling and more. The only actual positive result was the easier training. Now overweight and underpowered, the Observation Type 2 immediately acquired less flattering sobriquets. First it was the Oscar Deuce, but soon became known as the Oscar Duck, then the Ruptured Duck. Those were the kinder terms. Less flattering names such as Push Me/Pull You, Sky Smasher, Sky Pig and Pilot Sandwich evolved; the latter in morbid reference to the fore and aft engines with pilot and fuel between. Crash, and the result is a pilot sandwich – toasted.

But this O-2 carried its two crewmembers safely aloft. Blake had Rusty fly around the entire area of the brigade's operating zone, pointing out known friendly areas and known enemy ones. The latter far outnumbered the former, Blake emphasized, and the designation was apt to alternate from day to day. Rusty duly noted both types on his satchel-full of large-scale maps. Blake hardly touched the controls, taking them over only when he wanted to give Rusty the chance to devote his full attention to something on the ground, or when Rusty was taking detailed notes on his maps. He was doing just that when Blake quietly said, "Rusty, you have the plane."

Rusty quickly tucked the map under his right thigh, took the controls and replied, "Roger, I have it."

They were flying over the end of a rocky escarpment, the last finger of basaltic flow from a prehistoric volcano. Blake said, "Roll to the right. You see that little clearing there? The one with the basalt flow on this side and the tree line on the far side?"

"Uh huh."

"An do you see those white flashes coming from the edge of the tree line? That twinkling?"

"Uh huh. Why?"

"You know what that twinkling is?"

"Um, reflections of the sun off wet leaves? No, wait. The sun is at the wrong angle to cause reflections like that. Besides, those aren't moving along with our path like they would if they were reflections. I give up, what are they?"

"Ground fire."

Rusty jerked the yoke in sudden panic. "Ground fire? You mean we're being shot at?"

"That's right," Blake said calmly. "Small arms only. Probably AK-47s judging from the small flash and the number of rounds fired at a time: they use 30-shot clips, you know. Looks like maybe five gomers. A patrol, probably. FNGs like you, certainly. An experienced group or one with a decent non-com along wouldn't have opened fire at a FAC. That tends to be suicidally stupid."

Rusty tore his eyes off the evil white flashes and looked at Blake. "How can you sit there and play Sherlock Holmes when those guys are trying to kill us?" Rusty blurted.

"Oh, we're in no danger. Or almost none. We're almost completely out of range, and those gomers are so green they're probably aiming right at us – and missing by hundreds of feet behind us as a result. Nah, we could damn near hover here and still be safe. Even if we could hover in this sky pig. Of course, even a hovering pig isn't kosher," Blake chuckled to himself.

"Shouldn't we call in an airstrike? Or artillery? Or something?" Rusty babbled, almost as fast as a two-year-old.

"Well, we could do either or both of those things. But to be honest, in the 20 minutes or so that it would take to get assets here, those gomers will have run more than a mile. Even ones dumb enough to shoot at a FAC will soon come to their senses, or a more senior troop will. Then they'll dee dee mau right now," Blake paused to savor the unintentional rhyme. "And by the time we have fighters overhead – possibly diverting them from a genuine valuable target – there'll be nothing down there but innocent trees. Instead, you show me how well you can read that map, and plot the exact coordinates of where they were. Repeat were, because you'll note they've already stopped firing."

28

Despite his thudding heart, Rusty reverted to his training. Orienting his map with North upwards, he first compared the relationship of their general position with distant but visible landmarks, then the broad outline of the basalt ridgeline, and finally the detailed topographical contours of that one clearing. By working from large to small scale, he was soon able to write down a set of coordinates that would locate the location of the groundfire to within about one hundred meters.

"Very good, indeed. Very good thinking about the sun angle initially, by the way, and not only that but you are correct about the map coordinates. Plus, you managed to keep from crashing the plane while you found them. I'm pleasantly surprised. Either the FAC school at Hurlburt is much improved or you are a talented student of FACkery." Blake grinned at Rusty. "Now we'll see if you can hit Mother Earth with a rocket. Why don't you set up a marking pass and see how close to that clearing you can get with a Willie Pete."

"We get to shoot back, huh?" Rusty grinned as he turned the O-2 first away from the clearing and then back in a climbing, rolling, twisting path that ended up with the nose of the plane pointing steeply down and right at the clearing. Snapping the armament switches to 'Fire' and then pressing the tiny red button in his yoke, Rusty launched a supersonic 2.75-inch rocket known as Willie Pete for the white phosphorous inside its warhead. With a sudden WHOOSH, it raced away from under their right wing, arching down and exploding with a plume of brilliant white smoke only a few meters from the edge of the clearing. But hardly had the rocket cleared its pod when Rusty had smoothly pulled the plane out of its steep dive, added power and made another twisting, corkscrew turn.

"Again, you astound me, Rusty. You not only managed to place your rocket somewhere in this hemisphere, but you avoided following it into the same hole while watching it fly. Truly rewarding. Who knows, you may even have hit one of the murdering sons of Satan, may they all be damned to hell."

"I thought the existence of hell was not a tenet of faith among Jews," Rusty said, grinning after the snide compliment.

"Among Jews who have not been to Vietnam, perhaps that is true," Blake said, wistfully. "But I have seen hell with my own eyes, Rusty, and it is right under our wings."

Neither of them spoke for a few minutes, except for Blake to direct Rusty to find the home field and fly there. They were almost ready to land when Rusty asked, "Do I pass?"

Blake chuckled. "Well, I know that you can fly, and navigate, and read a map, and even shoot rockets. Which, as I intimated, is promising. So you're almost there. Tomorrow, we'll see how you conduct an air strike. That's another jar of gefilte fish altogether. It's even more harrowing than the practice strikes you flew at Hurlburt."

"But we worked with actual fighters there. Our IPs said it was as near to the real thing as they could create."

"Oy vey! They use live armament at Hurlburt now? They fill the airwaves with people jabbering on all three radios while you're trying to hear and talk on at least two of them? They shoot live ammo at you meanwhile?" Blake turned to Rusty. "I don't think so. If I'm not mistaken, today was the first time you've ever been shot at. You didn't even know what muzzle flashes looked like much less what kind of weapon might be creating them. You've never felt the blast and concussion of 500-pound bombs going off right under you. You've never had some poor bastard on the ground screaming to have the fighters drop ON his position because the enemy is that close. You've never had strike clearance cancelled on you while bombs are actually falling. You've never had to watch hundreds of enemy soldiers blithely give you the finger because they're standing in a no-bomb zone. Rusty, I assure you: ALL of those things will happen to you here, not once but over and over again. And I also assure you that no training you've received will or can prepare you for it. But tomorrow, we will see if you possess the rudimentary skills to do all that. Or not. Now land this pig and let's have a beer."

"It's horrible beer."

"Well then, it's highly appropriate for LZ Emerald."

They landed, and a different enlisted man pinned their rockets to safety and followed them back to their protective revetment. As they taxied, Blake said, "Our four enlisted slaves are Richards, Smith, Washington and Gomez. Their ranks are unimportant, except that Richards is senior. They're all the best of the best, but if you ever have a problem of any kind with one of them, you go through Richards to handle it. Never, ever reprimand one of the others directly or you'll cut the ground right out from under Richards. They're HIS troops. Copy?"

"Yeah, I copy that. What if I have a problem with Richards?"

"Then you go through me. But it had better be a genuine Adolf Hitler of a problem, because quite frankly, Richards is more valuable to me than you are."

"That's weird. When I had just landed at Cam Rahn, one of the first guys I met was a sergeant in a jeep, and he used almost those exact words: that he was more valuable than a pilot. I'm beginning to believe it."

"Do believe it. If there's one thing they should teach lieutenants, it's this: Never, never, never doubt a senior non-com. If one of them tells you the rain will fall UP today, you do not argue. You stand inside your umbrella."

Rusty laughed at the image, but he took the words to heart.

They arrived back at the FAC Shack to find Crazy Eddie sunbathing outside – stark naked - and Brian inside reading a paperback. "Bob is up running one of the long-range patrols. More on that later," Blake said. "And Brian is scheduled to fly a VR mission later today. Once you're on the team – assuming you make the grade – you can expect to fly once a day, almost every day. There are four of you and only three planes, one of which may be on a parts run or something, so we try to fly each plane twice a day. Aircraft availability is really the main limit on how much flight time you'll get, but you'll get plenty. Any questions for now?"

"Just one. You said we'll fly an airstrike tomorrow? How do you know?"

"Good question. Airstrikes are either pre-planned or emergency. Let's say that Brian is up looking for targets today. While he's up there, one of the brigade patrols gets ambushed and they call for air. That request would go up the chain of command and back down again, and he'd be assigned a set of fighters, or several, and he'd work them right then and there. The same would happen if he found a lucrative but temporary target like troops in the open or a moving truck. Got it?"

"Yup, those are obvious."

"But he's more likely to find a target that seems valuable but isn't going anywhere. Maybe he sees stacks of crates and barrels camouflaged under some trees, or a bunker complex. He plots them, reports them and the Olympian powers that be analyze them at leisure. They prioritize them, run them past all the political and tribal leaders; then, if everyone agrees to hit them, they schedule fighters with the appropriate weaponry and plan a mission down to the last detail. It comes down to us as a small part of that day's entire air war schedule, which is why they're called frag orders, not for fragmentary bombs but because that mission is a fragment of the whole picture. That's a pre-planned strike, and we have one that's been providently assigned to us for tomorrow. Crazy Eddie found it, but I'm going to let you hit it. I'll break the bad news to him."

He did, and Crazy Eddie seemed to take the disappointment with only a shrug. "Oh well, what's one airstrike more or less? I was looking forward to hitting that one, though. It might be a plum."

"Thanks for taking it that way, Eddie. I'll give you a target of my own if I find one some day."

"See that you do. If you don't, it'll drive me crazy."

"Drive? From what Bob and Brian tell me, that wouldn't even be a short putt."

Crazy Eddie erupted into a weird, hooting wail so loud and eerie that it disconcerted Rusty.

"Don't do that to a new guy without warning, Crazy Eddie," Blake said. To Rusty, he said, "That's just Crazy Eddie's laugh. If you can apply the qualifier 'just' to such a frightening fusillade of tympanic tempestuousness."

"Oh, my. I don't know which is more surprising: Crazy Eddie's laugh or your facility with words. I thought I had a pretty good vocabulary as an English Major, but I don't think I could have come up with a sentence like that off the cuff. I'm duly impressed, sir," Rusty said.

Blake looked vacantly at the sky in mock humility, "Oh, well. We Jews are supposed to be highly educated, you know. I have to hold up the image, is all."

"I thought we Catholics were the ones who hold up images. Graven ones, according to some," Rusty shot back.

Blake gave him an appreciative sidelong look. "You may do on acumen alone, Naille. Gentlemen, I do not recommend a duel of wits with our new arrival here. He's the only one in this shack who seems to be armed."

All three of them laughed at that.

Later that afternoon, as the mandatory officers' cocktail hour approached, Rusty asked about the FAC Shack's curious shower. "I suppose it's close enough to Saturday night to start thinking about a bath, guys. How's that shower contraption work?"

Brian looked up from his book. "Yeah, close enough for me, too. Hang on and I'll get the ladder."

"Ladder? You need a ladder to take a shower?"

"Well, not exactly. But you do need one for a *hot* shower. Follow me."

He led Rusty outside, where he leaned a homemade wooden ladder up against the wall of the hooch. When they'd both climbed up, Brian revealed the secrets of the water heater.

"See, it's an immersion heater," he said. "There's a doughnut-shaped chamber there at the bottom of that garbage can. This small tank here drips fuel – and it'll burn almost anything from diesel to rocket fuel – into the chamber through this pipe. Air also passes down the pipe, and smoke comes up this other one. The fuel burns in the circular chamber. As it does, the water gets hot. We rigged up this toilet valve and float to keep the garbage can full. That pipe there leads water down to the shower head."

"That's brilliant! An underwater fire!" Rusty exclaimed. "Who invented that?"

"Beats me. It's apparently a commercial design. The immersion heater is, at any rate. It's been here as long as I have, but I was told an earlier FAC bought it and flew it in here. Before that, they had had to clean up out of a shaving basin. Then other FACS kept improving it with the stall, water supply, and finally the toilet valve. We still have to climb up here to fill the fuel tank and light the thing, though. I don't know how we could get around that."

"Hmmm. Nor I – at the moment. Speaking of that, how do you light it?"

"Simple," said Brian. "You open this little valve here just a tiny bit. You want no more than a drop a second or thereabouts. As soon as possible after that, you just drop a lit match down here. Like this..."

Brian twisted the valve, looked down the intake pipe at the drips of fuel, then struck a match and dropped it in. There was a muffled WHOOMP and a perfect gray-white smoke ring poofed out of the chimney pipe. "And that's about it. In ten minutes, the water will be hot enough to use, and the toilet valve will automatically refill the garbage can with cold water. The first guy lights it and the last guy refills the fuel tank and shuts it off. Like I said: simple."

"Magnificent is what it is. I can't wait to try it."

"Yeah, I can't wait for you to try it out, either," Brian said, waving one hand in front of his face. "Wheeoo!"

"Oh, all right," Rusty said, returning Brian's silly grin, "make fun of the new guy. "

"One more day and you'd have been the *PHEW* guy," Brian said, leaping for the ladder.

All four of them showered in turn, changed and strolled up to the colonel's patio together. As they walked, Rusty asked, "It's beginning to dawn on me how important little things can be out there. That shower, for example. I can't even begin to imagine what else I used to take for granted and that I'll wish I had here."

"Uh huh," Crazy Eddie said. "My parents went through the Depression, and my Mother always talks about it. She must have told me a thousand times what they used to say: 'Make do or do without.' I never understood what that meant until I got here. But it's how we get along. We beg, we borrow, we barter. I won't say we 'steal' but we do know how to 'requisition' the things we need. That means everything from soap to rocket pods."

"Whattaya mean 'soap'," Rusty asked. "We can't buy soap here?"

"Well, in theory we can. The Army runs a PX. But they never have anything like that. They stock the place with the standard Army list of PX personal items. But they're always out of everything except tampons. They claim they can't order more men's personal items until they sell all the women's stuff, but there aren't any women on LZ Emerald. It's some kind of package deal, I guess."

"So why don't they just say they're out of everything and order another package?"

"They used to. That's why they now have full shelves of tampons and no shaving soap," Brian said.

"Can't they burn them or lose them or something? Heck, why don't we just buy all the tampons ourselves and just burn them?"

"We tried that. They won't sell tampons to guys. There's a regulation against it or something. They can't sell them, and they have to account for them so they refuse to throw them out. The only solution may be to burn the place down and then requisition a new PX," Crazy Eddie concluded.

"Hell, I wish they'd just bring in a few hundred women. That'd solve a lot more problems than too many tampons in the PX," Bob added.

"Oh yeah," Crazy Eddie swooned, "roundeyes. I think I remember roundeyes…ummm. White skin, smooth legs, white teeth…"

"Hey, yeah, that reminds me. I saw a Vietnamese woman right after I landed at Cam Rahn, and her teeth were black. Not just gray like they were bad teeth, but shiny, coal black! What the hell was that about?"

"Ah, Rusty, that's how you can tell a chewer of betel nuts. They chew the nuts for the mild narcotic effect, but the things stain their teeth black. It's permanent, too, I hear. Strange looking, huh?"

"It goes past strange, Bob. I thought it was positively Satanic. I hope I don't see any more like that."

"You might, though. It's pretty common, especially out in the villages. Betel nuts, marijuana, heroin, cocaine, you name it. But the locals don't use the really hard stuff much, except for some marijuana or opium smokers. They'd rather push the hard stuff on GI's." Brian chimed in.

The four had reached the colonel's patio, where martinis were being poured for everyone who arrived. "Thank goodness none of us ever ingest anything that would impair our flying skills," Crazy Eddie said, his voice dripping with irony as he accepted a full tumbler of

36

nearly straight gin. "The Army and Air Force would sure frown on behavior like that."

They sipped their drinks, but Rusty was the only one who even half enjoyed the gin. Whitworth and Blake were being buttonholed by a few Army officers of equal rank, and didn't get to meet with the FACs until they convened at their table. When they did, Whitworth leaned across and said to them, "I need to talk to you four, but not now. Blake and I will come down to the FAC Shack later this evening. Okay?"

"Yeah, sure, sir," Bob said. "We have nothing planned."

"Bob, you cannot pretend to forget our annual Summer Cotillion and Tea Dance, can you?" Crazy Eddie said, pooching out his lower lip in a pout. "The orchestra, the caterer, the dozens of debutantes; they'll all be simply crushed to hear you describe them as nothing."

Whitworth chuckled involuntarily, but recovered quickly and said, "Can it, Palmer. Blake and I will be down sometime later. Be decent for a change."

Blake turned to Rusty and said in a stage whisper, "Lt Palmer has a penchant for lounging about as God made him, as you may have noticed. With that hair, and that skin, not to mention his build, he is reminiscent of a shoe polish swab; and seeing a penile appendage on a KIWI swab is disconcerting…even if it is circumcised."

All six of them howled loud enough to bring disapproving stares all the way from the head table.

When Whitworth and Blake came down to the FAC Shack an hour or so after dinner, Crazy Eddie was wearing a flight suit over his fatigues, and had a bathrobe tied over all that. To Crazy Eddie's clear disappointment, neither man so much as batted an eye.

"What I didn't want to say aloud at the dinner table was that things don't seem to be going well for the Army right now. They haven't found so much as an enemy footprint in more than a week.

Needless to say, the colonel's daily action reports have been singularly lacking in action. His higher-ups are unhappy, and that makes the colonel very, very unhappy."

"So what does that mean for us?" Brian asked. "Are we supposed to fake enemy sightings or something just to bolster Napoleon's reports?"

"No, no," Blake jumped in, "But the colonel's fuse is even shorter than usual right now. We need to be professional and not give him a reason to blame the Air Force for anything."

"Meaning the major," Bob whispered to Rusty.

"Meaning *all* of us," Blake said, flushing slightly pink.

"I'm not the issue, Bigelow. As ALO, I'll handle any deserved criticism of our efforts here," Whitworth added, primly. "But I'd also prefer that we not deserve any. I'm not suggesting that we fabricate anything or even pad anything just to boost the brigade's record. I'm just asking for you four to be a little extra diligent in your work. I want good solid intel reports from all of you, whether that means you found enemy activity or you didn't. Negative findings are important, too. The Army will be greatly increasing their activities in the local area starting immediately. In addition, they'll be sending out extra patrols over the next few weeks, and they'll need solid and attentive overhead support – just in case. That's our job and I intend for us to provide it to the best of our ability. As soon as Naille here is fully qualified – hopefully with that airstrike tomorrow – we'll be at full strength. Captain Blake will be scheduling all of you hard. That's why I'm here, to let you know why."

"Just remember that the enlisted guys will be working even harder than you," Blake said. "So no complaints from you four. Hear?"

Rusty nodded at that, and said, "I'm here to fly. I just hope I can be a help to you guys."

"Never fear, Rusty. Just try to be a better FAC than Eddie here," Blake said as he and the major headed for the door. Over his shoulder, he added, "You already have him sweating."

All three turned to look at Crazy Eddie, who had rivulets of sweat running out of his incredible explosion of hair and down his face. As soon as the screen door slammed, he jumped up and tore off every stitch of the many layers he was wearing. Then, completely naked and glistening wet, he flopped back down into the chair. "I thought they'd never leave."

In the morning, they checked the flight schedule posted in the TOC.

"Well, Whitworth was serious," Bob said. "Looks like we're all scheduled to single bang one day and double-bang the next. Six missions total every day."

"Blake wasn't kidding about the poor enlisted guys. They'll be busting butt to keep that schedule with three planes," Brian agreed. "They won't be getting much sleep, that's for sure."

"Your preplanned strike is on for sure, Rusty. You have an oh-lunch-thirty takeoff in the plane I have. I'll be doing an early morning VR mission. You want me to swing past the strike site and do a last-minute look at it?" Eddie said.

"Uh, I don't know. Would that be a good idea or not?"

"Maybe yes and maybe no," Brian answered. "He found the place, so Crazy Eddie would be the best to check on any change in the site. He could confirm it's still valid, or maybe even a better target than before. On the other hand, a last-minute check might also alert the gomers that they've been found. That wouldn't be good."

"Up to you," Crazy Eddie said to Rusty, shrugging.

"I can see both sides of it," Rusty said after deliberating a few seconds. "But if we're going to hit that spot anyway today, it seems like it wouldn't add anything to know more about it, but it might be counter-productive. So, if you don't mind, I'd rather you didn't, Eddie."

"Fine by me. Just do a good job on it. 'Cause if you don't, I'll have to go back and do the job right – and repeat strikes tend to get hairy."

"How's that?"

"Oh, they are clever little bastards. You go back the next day, and they'll have moved out all the lucrative target stuff and replaced it all with heavy-duty anti-air guns. They hate FACs in general, but they'd be particularly pissed for getting hit once. They'd hammer a FAC big time on a second strike."

"Ah. I see. But can they really move stuff in and out that fast? I mean if they have tons and tons of ammo and fuel and food and stuff stacked in a spot, can they really replace it all with anti-aircraft guns overnight? I don't think we could do that, and we have aircraft and helicopters and trucks and more."

"Yeah, they can. They have trucks and cargo bicycles, too. But the big thing is they have a hundred bodies to every one of us, with unlimited bodies to call on if those aren't enough. Even if they had to lug it off one crate at a time on somebody's back, there's no shortage of backs. Believe me. Hey, I could go on about this for hours, but I have to make that first takeoff time." Crazy Eddie turned and loped off.

"Cripes, me too," Bob said, also running off.

Rusty turned to Brian. "He isn't all that crazy is he? I mean; those were some pretty clever insights."

"Oh, he likes to act weird, but there's a brain under all that hair…somewhere. But what he said isn't much different than any experienced FAC could tell you. Hell, you'll be spouting gems of FAC lore yourself by the time your replacement shows up. We're creating the FAC mission as we go, you know. We're the pioneers at it – just like Rickenbacker and Richthofen pioneered fighter tactics."

"That's heady company. I wonder who'll go down in history as the FAC equivalents to men like that."

"Who knows? Maybe you or Bob. Or me," Brian said, grinning. "Or Crazy Eddie."

"We three, maybe," Rusty kidded. "But not Crazy Eddie. Those fighter legends were all handsome and photogenic, after all."

Rusty spent the next two hours poring over the bag of maps that had been left to him by the FAC he was replacing. Brian filled him in on what the location of the upcoming airstrike looked like: a flat, lightly vegetated area in the broad half-circle of a river bend. It was maybe a half-mile long and a quarter wide, but a trace of dirt road ran through it. It was apparently one of the final capillaries in the huge circulatory system known as the Ho Chi Minh trail. Thousands of tons of war materials moved down that trail system, mainly by night. From huge supply depots in China and from major ports like Haiphong Harbor in North Vietnam came Russian and Chinese ammunition and guns, bedding and bandages, mines and mortars, rockets and rice. It wound its way down torturous paths through Laos and Cambodia – officially neutral countries whose governments could not or chose not to interfere with North Vietnam's single-minded goal: conquering the South.

"It's only the single-canopy tree cover that made it discoverable, you know. If they'd parked all that stuff under double or triple-canopy cover, even Crazy Eddie would never have found it. It's very well camouflaged, though. You may not see anything at all when you get there," Brian said.

Rusty raised his eyebrows in disbelief.

"No, that's not a dig at you or your abilities. But it's true, nonetheless. It takes time and experience to see the little details that act like clues. They don't exactly stake out big orange arrows that point to their supply depots. The average person wouldn't see anything there at all. But a wet spot on a riverbank, a clump of wilted leaves, a spray of new mud…they all add up to a hidden truck," Brian said.

"Explain that, will you?"

"Sure. When a truck crosses a stream, it naturally drips a lot of water onto the bank. Find a shallow spot with one bank all wet, and you know not only that something crossed there, but about how recently – and in which direction. Follow the dirt trail a bit and if you find mud sprayed out, that's a spot where the truck got stuck and spun its wheels. Again, you get a feel for how recently, plus a confirmation of which direction it was going. Then, you find a clump of trees where a lot of the leaves are wilted or turned up the wrong way. Right under that clump is your truck – with newly-cut limbs piled over it."

"Ah HAAA! I get it! Why didn't they ever tell us stuff like that back at Hurlburt?"

"Well, maybe the instructors never worked the Trail. Maybe they were FACs down in the Mekong delta. Or maybe they just couldn't verbalize the things they learned. Not all IP's are chosen for their teaching skills, you know. Were all your IP's in flight school great teachers?"

"Uh, no. I can't say they were. They were all great pilots, or nearly all. But not all of them could really teach. Some of them seemed like they just repeated a canned speech, no matter if that speech seemed to make sense to me or not," Rusty had to admit.

"Bingo. A great teacher is like a great musician: you don't always know why, but you know that what you're hearing is special. In fact, the better he is the less likely you are to notice how great they really are."

"Yeah, when you put it that way, I see exactly what you mean. Hey, I bet you'd be a great instructor, Brian."

"Thanks. You don't know how big a compliment that is. I don't think I admire anyone as much as a great teacher – no matter what he teaches."

"Let's go see how good your instructors were," said Blake, peering in through the screen door.

"Oh, Geez. I didn't hear you walk up!" Rusty said, startled. "OK, just give me a second to grab my stuff." He folded the map he was studying and put it back in its indexed place in the map bag, checked the pockets of his flight suit for all his gear and then slipped on his sunglasses.

"I guess that's it. I'm ready. Or I hope I am." They chatted as Blake drove them downhill from the hooch to the flightline.

"Relax. You'll do fine, Rusty. This isn't a real checkride. Mostly, I want to see what your style is and how you perform under actual combat conditions. Real weapons and a real enemy makes things go differently than those canned scenarios back at Hurlburt, you know. Even the in-country orientation at Cam Rahn doesn't give new FACs the full flavor of things."

"Sure gave me the full smell of things, though," Rusty joked – a bit nervously.

"Ah yes, the Cam Rahn bouquet is certainly memorable. Who was your orientation pilot there?"

"Major Spring," Rusty answered, but wondered why Blake had asked. Surely he'd read through Rusty's training folder and would have seen his IP's comments and signatures, right?

"Uh huh. Thought so. So you aren't an Academy grad."

"No. ROTC," Rusty said. So he'd been right about Spring, he thought to himself.

"Well, you may not regret your fate after all. Your school and your source of commission may have gotten you to LZ Emerald via the infamously biased Major Spring, but you may eventually come to appreciate it. You may get to see more real FACing here than you might have at a big base. You'll certainly get more sorties and maybe even more flight time here, too," Blake said, and turned his head to look at Rusty from the corner of his eye. "You may even get your knuckles metaphorically skinned from fighting courtesy of a knuckle knocker." Blake lifted one corner of his lip in a wry half-smile.

When they pulled up in their jeep, Crazy Eddie was filling in the aircraft's Form 781, the flight and maintenance log that told the condition of the plane. "All green, Captain Blake. She's good to go as soon as Sgt Gomez gets her gassed up. I didn't fire any rockets. Knew you'd be needing them. Just check the left seat cushion before Rusty straps in."

"Uh huh. I'll do that." Blake and Rusty elbowed their way into their survival vests and leaned their parachutes and helmets against the plane's right main gear tire while they both made a careful walk-around inspection. After they'd checked everything that could be examined from the outside, they donned the 'chutes and helmets and prepared to board.

Blake peered in ahead of Rusty. "Yup, left seat cushion okay."

Rusty wrinkled his brow in confusion, but said nothing. There was nothing in the checklist about verifying the seat cushions. Nor could he imagine why Crazy Eddie and Blake had thought it necessary. He swung up and across the right seat, almost falling into the left one.

"Damn! Crazy Eddie has the seat all the way back against the stops. Is he really that tall?" Rusty struggled to unlatch the seat lock and slide it forward, the task made more difficult because when at rest on the ground, the cabin tilted up a bit. Lurching hard to fight gravity and the added weight of his parachute and reinforced Kevlar helmet, Rusty finally got the seat adjusted for his average height and leg length. "Whew! I'm sweaty already after that."

"Well, you'll likely be a bit damper when you climb out again. Let's get fired up, we don't have much time to get out to the target before the fighters arrive, and they'll have even less gas than we will."

"Roger that, sir. I'm about done with the checklist. Ready to start."

Rusty started both engines while Sgt Gomez watched with a fire extinguisher. Blake sat silently while Rusty got the radios turned on and tuned: there were three communications radios and two navigation sets to check. But before Rusty asked for taxi and takeoff instructions, Blake asked him, "You do have all the frequencies and TACAN fixes, right?"

"Yessir, right here," Rusty patted his leg board. "Updated with today's freqs and callsigns, plus the daily codes."

"Good. What's the fighter call sign – from memory?"

Without looking down at his leg board, Rusty said, "Playboy Two Six, flight of two F-4s. They'll be on UHF 236 point six."

"Very good. Okay, let's hit it."

Rusty got takeoff clearance, winds and the current barometer setting for the altimeter, and taxied to the runway where Sgt Gomez armed his rockets. Handing the safety pins and red streamers to Rusty through the small pilot's weather window, Sgt Gomez leaned close and shouted, "Hit 'em hard, sir!"

"Everybody knows everything around here," Blake lamented. "I wouldn't be surprised if the damned NVA doesn't get the frag orders at the same time we do."

"Is it really that bad?"

"Not really, but sometimes it seems so. No time to bemoan that right now, though. After we get airborne, turn right out of traffic. The Army helicopter pads are on the other side of the LZ, and they make their landing circuits to the west. We make ours on the east side to reduce the conflicts. But keep your eyes peeled anyway. They don't always follow any protocols at all."

"Eyes peeled. Right turn it is." Rusty retracted the landing gear and flaps, looked warily in all directions, then rolled into a right turn out of the traffic pattern.

"Which way is the target zone?" Blake quizzed.

"Southwest. So I'll climb up and make a long turn that way. It's only about ten miles out, so I won't bother with a TACAN nav fix. I'll navigate by map."

"Good; that's preferable anyway. The better you learn the area the better FAC you'll be. And there's no better way to learn it than by looking at the ground to navigate."

Before they'd even completed the long climbing turn, Rusty said, "Okay, there's the big bend in the river right there. The target zone should be right there on this side of it, along the inside of that big bend." A few minutes later, they were almost overhead. "I won't fly right over it, or start an orbit just yet. Don't want to alert them to what's coming," Rusty said as he checked the UHF radio frequency was set to the fighter's frequency, the VHF radio was dialed to their own TOC and their TACAN navigation radio was tracking the nearest ground station.

"How about the VHF-FM set?" Blake asked him.

"Well, there aren't supposed to be any friendlies patrolling in this area, but I'll dial in the daily working freq anyway, just to be safe. I'll keep the volume down a little, though."

Blake nodded. "Excellent. Somebody taught you well."

At that moment, there was a click and they heard "Playboy Two Six...Two." It was their pair of fighters checking with each other after they changed frequency. Rusty waited, and then heard, "Uh Baggy Oh Four, Playboy Two Six up your push."

"Copy you loud and clear, Playboy. This is Baggy Zero Four with you. Mission number is..." Rusty looked at his leg board, "Bravo, niner, two, seven, delta, niner."

"Copy and confirm, Baggy. We're at angels two two, twenty minutes of play time, lead has four Mark 82 snakeye and four CBU. Two has eight nape and we both have gun. Ready for your brief."

Rusty quickly scribbled down the pertinent info in grease pencil on his left window, plus the time. Then, "Roger Playboy, are you at the fix?"

"Affirmative, Baggy. And we have you in sight. Confirm with rock."

Rusty rocked his wings steeply from side to side then held his turn to the left.

"Tally ho, Baggy. Have you rocked and now left. Ready to copy."

"Playboy, your target is a storage area with probable troops. Small arms only expected. Best bailout is feet wet, east. Nearest emergency field is Phu Cat, forty miles southeast. You may use random attack from a wheel. Terrain is flat and target elevation is 200 feet MSL. No friendlies in the area. Winds seem to be calm. FAC will orbit east at two thousand. Over."

"Copy all, Baggy. Cleared to come down and wheel?"

Rusty craned his neck and looked above him all around. Suddenly, he spotted two black trails and followed them forward to their source: two mottled-green F-4 Phantom jets flying in loose formation. "Ah, tally on you Playboy, you are cleared to descend to best altitude and set up your wheel. Say when you're ready for a mark."

"Wilco, Baggy. Coming down. Two, wheel left."

"Two" came the reply from the wingman.

Everything was beginning to happen in a blur of activity and commotion, but Rusty took a deep breath and turned towards the target area. He still hadn't flow over it, but was angling closer with each second. He could see nothing down there but a thinly forested area with the faint hint of a two-track road through it. No enemy troops, no trucks, no stacks of crates or drums stood out. He stared hard to try to find some, but was interrupted within seconds.

"Baggy, Playboy is in wheel left. Mark it."

Unable to see anything definite, Rusty shrugged hopefully to himself and rolled the plane into his favorite maneuver: a rolling, climbing, twisting corkscrew that ended with his wings level and the nose pointing steeply down. He turned the arming switches to FIRE, let the glowing red dot of his heads-up sight slide along the ground until it was roughly in the center of the target zone, and then touched the switch in his yoke. WHOOSH went a four-foot-long rocket out of the left wing rocket pod. Immediately, Rusty pulled and turned the control yoke, smoothly adding power when the nose cleared the horizon. He reversed the roll and saw the bright white plume of smoke on the ground. "Playboy lead, call your direction and hit my smoke."

"Lead is in from the south with a pair of snakes."

Rusty snapped his head that way and saw the lizard-like colors of the jet as it plunged down. Lead's cleared hot." Rusty turned again, keeping the fighter in sight. Fascinated, he saw two sleek green shapes detach from the jet, and then four large petal-like fins popped open at the rear of each bomb. The metal devices slowed the bombs so they did not explode directly under the jet that dropped them, and they also caused the bombs to oscillate slightly in flight – exactly like the head of a cobra – hence their nickname: snakeye. As the jet climbed safely away, both bombs detonated in a flash of orange-red flame and dirty gray-black smoke. Rusty was surprised to see a white mushroom-like shock wave flash away from the explosions: the result of the shock wave on humid air. But before he could marvel at that, he heard, "Two is in east. FAC in sight."

Already falling behind in his tasks, Rusty managed to blurt out "Two, hit Lead's spot. Cleared hot." He craned his neck to find Two, but saw only the huge blossom of white-hot flames as two canisters of napalm ripped into the jungle floor. And then he saw something else,
48

dozens of little white sparkles coming from almost everywhere below him.

In an odd calm, he said, "Uh, Playboy, you're taking ground fire from the whole area. Small arms, probably AK-47. And hold your wheel for a second while I reposition. He'd drifted almost over the target trying to observe the bomb hits, and that was not a good place to be with jets dropping bombs in that same tiny bit of space.

"Playboy is holding dry. But they're not shooting at us, Baggy. You're the one they want today."

Rusty gulped involuntarily, and also yanked on the control yoke. He wanted to fly as unpredictably as possible to keep some VC gomer down there from drawing a bead on him. When he was off to the east again, he clicked his transmit button. "OK, Lead. If you have me in sight, call and make another run. Hit 100 meters south of your first impact."

"Lead's in north with a pair of snake, FAC in sight."

"Tally ho, and cleared hot," Rusty said. Again, he watched the jet plummet, the twin bombs pop open and wobble their ominous way to earth, then the huge twin blasts. This time, Rusty felt and heard the quick double BaBam of the shock waves. Readier this time, he scanned the sky and saw the wingman just as he rolled in. "Tally on your roll, two, hit another 100 meters south of lead and cleared hot." He heard the wingman click his radio button twice in a wordless signal that he'd heard and would comply.

The huge splash of jellied gasoline and naptha rolled silently through the trees, but before it burned out, Rusty saw first one then two additional explosions. "You got secondaries on that pass, two. Good job. Break. Lead, your next pass will be CBU, right?"

"That's affirm, Baggy. Where you want it? I can give you two more passes, then one with the gun."

"Two" said the wingman, confirming that he, too had enough fuel for three more runs on the target."

"Copy that, Playboy. Ok then, just blanket the area of two's last run. There may be more down there. I see muzzle flashes from there, too."

"Copy. Lead's in west with CBU. FAC in sight."

"Have you in sight also, Lead. FAC is clear and you are hot."

This time, two white canisters dropped from the jet, and almost immediately split apart. Rusty saw nothing else, but seconds later, an oblong area the size of a football field erupted with hundreds of white flashes and sparks. Several fires roared to life just as Rusty heard a strange but terrifying sound like a deep, menacing electrical buzz. Once again, he was almost mesmerized by the sight and sound, but was jolted back by the wingman.

"Two's in south with nape."

"Cleared hot, two. Hit anywhere near your last strike."

Twin silver canisters tumbled and winked their way to the ground. A hell of flames and angry black smoke rolled down through the treetops. And then, yet more explosions as something on the ground blew up.

Rusty noted fewer spots of muzzle flashes now, and he edged in to get a better look at Lead's final drop of cluster bombs. He knew that CBU canisters contained hundreds of baseball-sized bomblets each more powerful than a hand grenade, and designed to produce both lethal shrapnel and fire-starting incendiary fragments. It was the ideal weapon to use against troops and vehicles, and he wanted to get a close look at the results. He cleared Lead hot, and had just observed the twin canisters split open when he heard and felt a sharp "PANK" sound like someone had hit a garbage can with a hammer – and he'd been inside the can.

"That's a hit, Rusty. You're getting too low," Blake said, with an odd calm.

Rusty shot a glance at his altimeter and realized he'd let himself get down to only a thousand feet above the ground. He slammed the throttles full and started a twisting climb, missing the result of the bomb drop altogether, but hearing that electrical ripping sound of the bomblets going off again. Trying to recover his duties, he managed to spot the wingman start his final napalm pass, and cleared him hot. "Put 'em wherever it looks good," he said, unable to think of anything better.

"Playboy is ready for a gun run, Baggy. You OK down there?"

"Uh, yeah, I think so. Took a hit from something, but don't think it's a problem. Uh, can you just lay me a track of 20 mike mike through the area? I don't have a spot target, but the whole area seems active."

"Roger that, Baggy. Lead's in with gun, east."

Still climbing and turning, Rusty managed to see Lead's jet as a cloud of smoke enveloped it from below. Jerking his eyes to the ground, Rusty saw a line of white explosions almost as large as those from the cluster bombs. The explosions jumped and twisted around like a stream of water being played across the ground, but with opposite effect: fires and smoke sprung to life from several places. He cleared the wingman through for his gun pass, and still more ground explosions and fires leapt to life.

"Baggy, Playboy Two Six is Winchester and headed home. We'll copy your BDA when your ready, Baggy. Two, join up left. Switches safe." Click click.

Having reached a safer altitude, Rusty dug out his binoculars and flew an orbit around the target zone. Peering down, he was shocked to see burning crates of all sizes, ruptured and burning oil drums, a flaming truck and lots of unidentifiable but manmade debris. And then, as he looked closer, he was even more shocked to see bodies and parts of bodies laying in several places, blackened and still. He gulped and made quick grease pencil notes.

"Uh, Playboy, BDA as follows: 15 minutes on target. 100% good bombs, 100% on target. Target destroyed. Observed numerous secondary explosions and fires. One truck destroyed, numerous crates and oil drums destroyed. Numerous KBA observed. Um…real good work, Playboy."

"Shit on a stick work, Baggy. Copy all. That one goes in the diary. Drinks on us, anytime, anywhere, little brother."

Rusty stared straight ahead and shook himself, trying to catch up to the whirl of sights, sounds and emotions he felt. He suddenly realized he was pouring with sweat, and his heart was racing. His hands shook violently, and his feet were dancing on the rudder pedals with a life of their own. Blake said, "I have the aircraft."

Rusty tried to let go of the controls, but it took an effort to unbend his fingers to do it. "Uh, you have it."

Blake also reached across and took the binoculars from Rusty, then started a right turn and circled the target area again. He jotted down a few things on his own leg board, and then said to Rusty, "OK, you have it again. Take us back to LZ Emerald. I'll make the Bomb Damage Assessment report to the TOC myself. But first, let me ask you one question."

"OK"

"Are you seriously asking me to believe that you have never worked an airstrike before today? That that was your first time?"

"Uh, no. Or yes. I mean, it was. Why?"

Blake just shook his head for a moment, then said, "Because if that's true, then there's only one thing I can possibly say, and it's not a phrase a Jew uses."

What's that?"

"Jesus H Christ."

They got back on the ground, but Rusty's landing bordered on ugly. The aftereffects of his massive adrenalin rush left him with little fine muscle control at all, and his stomach was doing flip flops from the nausea it also caused. In the re-arming area, Sgt Gomez met them and noted that they'd only fired one smoke rocket. "Slow day after all, sir?" He looked disappointed.

"Not completely," Blake said to him after they'd shut down back at the revetment. "There's a hole somewhere you'll have to patch. And I suppose that grounds this bird until you give it a complete inspection."

"You took a heet, sir? Just one? Oh, that's a shame. I mean, um…" He stammered and attempted to explain, but Blake slapped him on the back.

"No offense intended or delivered, Gomez. I know what you meant."

The sergeant beamed back at Blake, his eyes gleaming with eagerness and pride. His plane had been to the fight and come home again. He pumped his fist in excitement as he circled the plane as eager as a child at Christmas to find the bullet hole.

"Ay, Chihuahua! Aqui! I mean, here, capitan. Right here. Through tail boom. Nutting in there but some wires. I patch it real quick. Fly again tomorrow. OK?" Gomez reverted to border Tex-Mex in his excitement.

"OK," Blake said. "But you check it out real good. I don't want to have a fire in there next time the lieutenant flies it, you hear?" He grinned at the man in mutual pleasure.

Rusty beamed inwardly. Next time I fly it? I must have passed muster!

"Oops, almost forgot," Blake said. "Sergeant, check that seat cushion again, will you?

"Oh, si!" Gomez ran around and leaned into the cockpit, then pulled his head out, a dour look on his face. "Si, it is ruined. Too bad." He made a tent with his hands.

"What is it with that seat cushion?" Rusty said to Blake, vaguely annoyed.

"Oh, we always check it before and after a new FACs first combat mission. Like most, you puckered your asshole so tight you sucked the cushion up. Yours looks like Mount Fuji. Poor Gomez will have to iron it back down flat. I think you owe your crew chief a drink."

Blake and Gomez collapsed into gales of laughter. Rusty laughed, too. "I think that might be arranged. With gratitude."

Blake drove straight to the TOC with Rusty. They walked into the building, and Rusty noted a narrow central corridor flanked with cubicles along each wall. They turned and walked almost to the rear, stopping outside a cubicle labeled S-2 Air. Rusty knew from his days at Air/Ground Operations School, or AGOS, that this was the Army's cryptic designation for the Air Intelligence Officer. Rusty was behind Blake, and could hardly see, but he did glimpse the occupant. Inside sat an acne-scarred captain in starched fatigues and brilliantly shined boots – clearly a man who spent no time whatsoever in the field, or even outdoors.

"You are hand delivering the BDA from that pre-planned strike, Captain Blake? Why?" The man said, suspiciously.

"Yes I am. I just wanted to see you read it."

The man frowned at that, and looked at the paper Blake had handed him. In seconds, he blanched, then went from white to beet red. "Are you playing jokes with me, Captain? Show me the real BDA."

"That *is* the real BDA," Blake said striving to, but unable to keep from grinning. "And I think you'd better present it to the Colonel ASAP."

Without a word, the man leapt up and bowled past them on his way to the private suite of offices at the far end of the corridor. In minutes, the door there opened a second time and the Intel officer emerged. A strange look was on his face, but he said, "The Colonel wants to see you immediately."

Blake turned to Rusty and said, "You come along, but don't say anything unless the colonel or I address you. Copy?"

Uh oh, thought Rusty. Maybe I'm in deep shit. Maybe I really screwed up somehow and Blake is going to try to defend me. Oh shit.

They stopped at attention before a huge mahogany desk flanked by US and unit flags – but no chairs except the one occupied by Colonel Ardmore. Before Blake could drop his salute and report, Ardmore was waving the BDA sheet in the air. "Blake. Goddamn you! What is this shit?"

"That is the BDA from a preplanned airstrike run less than an hour ago, Colonel. It reports…"

"I can bloody well read, Captain. But what kind of bullshit am I reading? Is this somebody's idea of a fucking joke? Because if it is, I'll have the son of a bitch court martialled tomorrow. No, today by God."

Rusty went cold and felt the blood drain from his face. Oh Lord, what kind of trouble am I in?

"There is no joke whatever, Colonel. I wrote that BDA myself. I was present at the airstrike myself and witnessed it." Blake said, coolly.

Ardmore rocked back in his heavily padded swivel chair as if he'd been punched, then leapt forward again. "I still say it's bullshit. I'm going to send a team out there to physically search the place, and so help me, if this isn't accurate, I'll…I'll…Hell, I don't know what I'll do, but it will NOT be a joke, either."

"I believe that to be an accurate BDA, Colonel, but it is difficult to get an absolutely accurate assessment while being fired at and while flying a plane. So that may be understated a bit."

"Understated? Did you say UNDERstated?" You claim to have destroyed more enemy material and killed more enemy troops than this entire brigade has achieved in a whole month, and you think your report may be a bit UNDERstated? You have some gall, to think that one Air Force captain can achieve results like that in one day."

"Ah, but perhaps I didn't make myself completely clear, Colonel. It wasn't one Air Force captain. It was one Air Force lieutenant. This man here. On his very first combat airstrike, I might add. In fifteen minutes…Sir."

"GET OUT OF MY SIGHT!"

"Thank you, sir," Blake said, saluting smartly and spinning crisply on his heel.

Rusty almost stumbled trying to simultaneously salute, do an about face and stay on Blake's heels. A light had begun to glow in his mind. Could it be?

Outside the door, Blake doubled up in silent laughter, tears streaming down both cheeks. He slapped his palms against his thighs and then clapped one hand over his mouth. Red-faced, he motioned Rusty to follow him and they hustled to the building where he and Whitworth had their offices - if you could dignify a pair of shattered desks and a few rickety chairs in a dungeon as offices.

"Frank, I should've radioed you with this, but it wasn't something I wanted to broadcast over open airwaves. You would not have believed it." He took a breath. "First, as you know, I was hoping Lt Naille would be a decent FAC. Hell, after reading his training reports, I almost dared to hope that he might be a good FAC. But Frank, I have to say he isn't."

"He's not?" Whitworth looked at Rusty, and disappointment showed deep in his eyes."

"No, he's not. He's an absofuckinglutely *great* FAC. I'm taking world-class, born natural, ace of aces, no shit, monster FAC. You should've been there. I still cannot believe what I saw, and I DID see it. Even Playboy Lead was impressed, and you know what dickheads those Playboy jocks are. They hadn't a clue it was a first mission. Not a glimmer. And the results? Oh my Lord in heaven, look at this."

Whitworth snatched the sheet from Blake's hand and his mouth dropped open. "Are you sure about these numbers?"

"I did that BDA myself. If anything, they're low. It wasn't a strike. It was a sledgehammer blow." Then Blake cocked his head a little as a thought struck him. "And this is the lad who... ahem... Nailled it."

Rusty didn't know whether to faint, pee his pants or simply stand there and grin like the village idiot. He managed two out of three...

CHAPTER THREE

Rusty was floating through an alcoholically enhanced erotic dream. The smoldering brunette with enormous tits bucking and groaning under him suddenly and inexplicably exploded, launching Rusty through the air. Before he could marvel at this, he landed with an all-too-real thud, only to have another body land on top of him.

"FUCK! Incoming!"

Rusty snapped to semi-consciousness in an instant, but his mind still reeled in the fog of a Black Label buzz. Incoming?

WHAM!

Oh, yeah, incoming, Rusty said to himself. Then, his mental fog beginning to clear, Oh shit! Incoming! He scrabbled on the floor, trying to get under his bunk. Just as he did, WHAM another explosion came, nearer than the last. The fluorescent light fixture dropped and exploded with a bang on the floor. Tiny bits of light tube glass stung Rusty's cheek, chest and arm. KABLAM came an even louder blast.

They huddled in the dusty, pitch-black hooch for another minute while small arms rattled and the LZ's mortar tubes fired constantly with their weird POONK sound. Illumination flares burst to life, casting ghostly, dancing orange shadows as they swirled and spiraled down under parachutes. Then came deeper, throatier explosions, BOOMissshh.

"That's outgoing," Brian's voice coughed out of the darkness. "155's I think."

"Good guess Sherlock, since that's all they have here," Crazy Eddie touted.

"Oh, go take a flying fuck at a rolling doughnut," Brian laughed.

58

"If that doughnut has tits, that's just what I was doing. Until she exploded, that is," Rusty slurred.

"Huh?" said Crazy Eddie.

"Yeah, say again Huh?" Bob added.

"Dream," Rusty said woozily, belching a little.

"I do believe our Red Baron is still a bit tipsy, guys. Serves him right," Crazy Eddie said, but not meanly.

"I think the gomers really do have it in for him. They must be trying to get even for Rusty's little aerial circus this morning. Maybe we should have him bunk somewhere else, in case they zero in on him," Bob mused.

"Yeah, I bet the Cong are royally pissed at Rusty. Or all of us. You think they know where we bunk down? I mean really," Brian asked.

"Wouldn't be a bit surprised. They seem to learn everything else. Hell, I bet Colonel Napoleon personally passed the map coordinates of the FAC shack to Ho Chi Minh. Did you see the glare he gave Rusty at Happy Hour? Holy shit, if looks could kill, we'd be packing Rusty's stuff up right now.'

"Christ, I've never seen the whole frigging patio go dead silent like that. Rusty walks on the stage, and you could hear a pin drop."

"Bob, I could hear Napoleon's brain sizzling. Man, if he disliked the Air Force before, he must loathe us now. What a BDA!"

"I can't grasp it myself, guys. I gave the fighters one BDA, but then Blake looked for himself and wrote up another one. I didn't see half of what he reported. But then, I didn't see anything at all before the strike. Just trees. Crazy Eddie, what the heck did you see out there?"

"Frankly, I didn't see much, either. I saw where they probably had a truck or two parked – there were fresh tire tracks leading into the trees in two places. But that's it. I hadn't a clue it might be a major ammunition and fuel dump. But they say it's still burning and exploding out there. Christ!"

Rusty tried to sit up in the dark and banged his head on the iron cot frame. "Ow! Where'd you hear that, Eddie?"

"One of the friendlier Army intel guys. They sent out a couple of Hueys to check on the place. They didn't believe Blake's BDA, either, he admitted. But when they got there, fires were still burning and things were still cooking off. They found bunkers, caches of ammo and fuel, burning trucks and bodies. Lots of bodies. So many that they were afraid they might be attacked, so they dropped a few satchel charges into some undamaged bunkers and dee-dee-maued out of there. When they got back, they reported that even Blake's BDA was low. It's been re-re-revised and sent up to higher headquarters – again. By the way, Rusty, Blake also called the Playboy guys and told them they'd been worked by a combat virgin. They refused to believe it, until Blake swore that he'd been along. Then they said they'd work with that Baggy Oh Four FAC if they were flying box kites over Hanoi."

"I'm speechless, Eddie. I wish now that you could have worked that strike. You found it, and look what it turned into. I'm embarrassed."

"Well, now I wish I could have worked it, myself. But this morning, I would also have bet that the place would be empty, the trucks long gone and nothing there but bored monkeys. Another day using jets and bombs to make toothpicks. Just shows to go ya. Hey Rusty, I confessed, so…how'd you know exactly what to hit?"

"Eddie, I hadn't a clue. I just threw down a rocket in the general area and said, 'Hit my smoke'. Lead did, and the whole damn jungle lit up, first with small arms fire and then with secondaries. I couldn't believe it, but that was my first real strike, so I somehow thought that was the way airstrikes are supposed to turn out. I gather now that results like that are unusual."

"Unusual? Hell, Rusty, they'll be talking about that strike at Hurlburt in the next war! It'll be the textbook example of a perfect airstrike!"

"Perfect airstrikes include taking a bullet in the boom? I hope not."

"You took a hit, too? I didn't know that," Bob said, sitting up very straight.

"Guess I forgot to mention it in all the other excitement. Yeah. Made a heck of a bang. Went right through the left boom. Missed everything inside and just made two holes."

"The left boom, huh?" mused Crazy Eddie. "So maybe what? Ten feet directly behind you? Which means at a hundred fifty knots or so, that gomer missed putting one up your pink little ass by...a few hundredths of a second?"

Rusty was glad it was still pitch dark in the hooch, because he turned suddenly white.

As they talked, the outgoing mortar and artillery fire slackened off – there had been no more incoming rounds after the first salvo. The four FACs climbed back into their dusty bunks. When dawn came, they were up and out to see what damage the attack had caused. At first, nothing seemed out of place. But a few dozen yards from the FAC Shack was a shallow crater. Closer inspection revealed new shrapnel holes in the sandbag wall around the hooch, and a piece of jagged, torn metal lay on the ground next to it.

"That's right next to your bunk, Rusty. Looks like they *were* aiming for you after all," Bob joked.

"Yeah, but at least they missed the two important things," Crazy Eddie said.

"Like what?"

"The shower and the four-holer, of course."

Brian put his hand on Rusty's shoulder and shook his head sadly, "Hate to say it, Rusty, but he's right. We can always get another FAC, even another crapper, but the shower...well..."

They joshed each other all the way to breakfast, where they found Whitworth and Blake already at the table, just finishing.

"Morning, all," Whitworth said. "You came through the festivities last night in one piece, I see."

"Yeah, we did," Brian said, "but the light fixture bought the farm again. It's terminal this time, I think. We'll have to scrounge another one somewhere."

"Then my news may not be so bad," Blake said.

"Oh, no. I had a feeling there'd be bad news," Crazy Eddie moaned. "OK, lay it on us."

"Well, it's actually a good news, bad news thing. The bad news is that the plane Rusty flew yesterday is Red X'ed. The holes in the boom might have weakened it structurally, so Cam Rahn wants to inspect and test-fly it. They can't send a structural repair guy and a test pilot up here to do it, so they want us to fly it down there. And the good news is that one of you gets to go to Cam Rahn for two days," Blake beamed.

"Uh huh. Let me get this straight," Crazy Eddie said, "The plane is unsafe and unflyable, so they want us to fly it to them so they can make it safe?"

"You got it. So...who wants to go to Cam Rahn?"

They looked at each other in silence. Finally, Rusty said, "Guys, I guess I should. I mean; I broke it. So I ought to be the one to get it fixed. Unless one of you guys wants to go lay on the beach for a day?"

"No thanks." "I pass." Bob and Brian said simultaneously. Eddie waved his palms in front of him.

"Looks like you win the vote, Naille. While you're there, maybe you can wangle a new light fixture, too. Have fun!" Whitworth said.

"Uh huh. When do I go?"

"No rush at all, my boy. You have a whole half-hour to get airborne," Blake said.

"You jest."

"I'm as serious as a heart attack. The sooner you get it there, the quicker they can work on it, and we really need that plane in service. Besides, the weather guys call for moderate turbulence later today, and that's not a good thing if the boom is damaged. So I want you airborne while the air is as still as a millpond. Meaning now."

"Can I at least get some breakfast?"

"They have food at Cam Rahn. Blake will drive you down to the flightline. Take some coffee if you like," Whitworth said.

"Gee, thanks, sir."

The other three FACs snickered. But they stopped when Blake, already standing, said, "You three might want to check today's flight schedule before you laugh too hard. With one plane and one pilot down, you'll be taking up the slack. Toodleoo!"

In the jeep, Blake said, "We'll swing by the hooch so you can pick up a change of uniform and your travel kit. I'll brief you on some special restrictions while we drive to the plane."

"Special restrictions?"

"Well, naturally. In theory, a Red X entry in the 781 grounds the plane, so the maintenance guys at Cam Rahn have to issue a one-time special authorization to fly it. That in turn entails some extra cautionary limitations. Run in and get your stuff."

When Rusty got back with a small bag, Blake went on.

"All right, the bullet hole is in the left boom. That's the better of the two, because all the control cables run through the right boom. The only things routed down the left boom are some electrical wires. One powers the rotating anti-collision beacon, so the first restriction for this flight is – you will not use it. The second is a bit trickier. The other wires in the boom control your elevator and rudder trim tabs. So you're going to have to fly without trimming. We'll set it at neutral before takeoff, and that'll be it. You'll have to hold yoke pressure the whole flight. Think you can handle that?"

"Sure. There's hardly any control pressure in the O-2 anyway."

"It's not a matter of muscle, it's a matter of habit. You probably hit the trim button unconsciously. All pilots do, it's ingrained in your habits long before your first solo. But this time, you can't risk it. A little vibration, a hot circuit, and you have a fire. See?"

"Ah. Yeah, I do. Can we pull the trim circuit breaker?"

"We will. That's an explicit part of the instructions. They want us to tape the trim switch, too. But I still want you to keep your thumb off that switch. Copy?"

"Uh huh. I copy. No sweat."

"I thought not. By the way, I was glad you volunteered for this. You showed both leadership and good ethics when you did."

"And if I hadn't?"

"Oh, you were going to be the one to go, no matter what," Blake grinned. "Like you said, you broke it…"

"I thought so."

"Then there's the matter of the colonel. You are not exactly the apple of his eye right now. You put his precious brigade in a bad light when you outdid their VC head count. So the less he sees of you for a few days, the better. Ergo: you go." He finished as they pulled up in front of the revetment.

"Full gear? Or are we trying to minimize weight?" Rusty asked.

"Both," Blake replied. "We have only the main tanks filled, we dropped both rocket pods, and you won't be carrying any cargo – as much as I'd love to ferry some bad parts and stuff down to Cam Rahn. But going without a parachute and vest might not display the finest forethought. Just in case…"

"Just in case the boom buckles in flight? Yeah. As if there'd be even an ice cube's chance in hell of getting out of an O-2 that's out of control, especially from the left seat. Nobody ever has."

"Nobody ever had a first airstrike like you did, either, Rusty. You may be living a charmed life. But that reminds me. The third flight restriction you have is absolutely no "G" load allowed; plus or minus. Keep it at one G, period."

"Um, that's not completely possible, you know. Even rotating for a climb adds a fractional positive G."

"That's physics. This is Vietnam. No G load. Smooth as a baby's butt. You got it?"

Rusty saluted with a sardonic look. "Roger, Wilcox. Over and out, sir."

Sgt Gomez was his crew chief again, and he looked only a bit anxious as Rusty did a careful walk around. When he got to the left boom, Rusty tried not to pay too much attention to the damaged area, but he did see that two squares of aluminum had been riveted in place over the bullet holes. Unable to resist, he tapped one and turned to Gomez, "You use enough rivets?"

With a sudden smile, Gomez nodded, "All I could fit in, sir. Nutting too good for Baggy FAC."

Rusty wondered at the irony in that. He recalled a comment one of his instructor pilots had made back on the first day of flight school, "Remember, everything you use for the rest of your flying career will be supplied by the lowest bidder." Sobering.

He strapped in and went through all the normal checklist items, but made double sure that two circuit breakers were pulled out instead of pushed in: Anti-Collision and Trim. With a chuckle, he noticed that the pilot's trim button had not only been taped into immobility, but a paper cup had been taped over that. "NO!" had been written in felt tip marker on the cup.

He cranked up the engines, ran the rest of his checks, and motioned for Gomez to pull his wheel chocks. With no rocket pods to arm, there was no need for Gomez to follow him out in the jeep, but Blake and he did, anyway. Probably want to be eyewitnesses to the crash. But I'll have the best view. Rusty thought, morbidly.

When he got takeoff clearance, he added power and gingerly swerved around the worst of the potholes. When he reached flying speed, he took a deep breath and eased the yoke back. As smoothly as glass, he lifted off and climbed straight ahead. He raised the gear and flaps, noting that he already had to hold forward pressure on the yoke. As the speed built, the pressure against his hand did, too. Not heavy, but insistent was his best guess at its intensity.

The plane seemed to climb of its own free will. Well, it's as lightweight as I've ever flown one, he thought. Less drag without the rocket pods, too. This would be a joy if I could do a few aerobatics. Too bad. He turned to the southeast and tuned in the TACAN navigation station at Cam Rahn. He hadn't climbed far when the needle swung solidly and locked, only a few degrees off his nose. A tiny bank and it settled dead ahead. Suddenly, he realized how vastly different this kind of flying was from his highly structured training. Not only was there almost no radio chatter, but he hadn't even had to file a flight plan. He could pick his own route, his own altitude and his own speed. Unbelievable.

66

When he tried to level off, the locked trim went quickly from an inconvenience to a trial. If he didn't hold firm forward pressure, the plane wanted to pitch quickly upwards. That would suddenly increase the G load, though. Not good. As the cruising speed built, it got worse. Finally, Rusty pulled back on the throttles to slow down.

He dialed in the TOC and Blake immediately answered. "How's it going, Rusty?"

"Well, I sure wish we'd dialed in a bit more nose-down trim from the start. I'm using a good amount of pressure on the yoke."

"What's your airspeed and altitude?" Blake shot back.

"I'm level at six, and I throttled back to just 120 knots. Steady as she goes for now. Cam Rahn dead ahead at 74 miles."

"OK, that sounds good. Can you hold it for a half hour?"

"Oh yeah. It's not heavy, just constant. The air is smooth and I haven't done any high-speed inverted whifferdills," he joked, naming an imaginary aerobatic maneuver.

"Good. See that you don't. Call back if anything changes, and have the TASS notify us when you're on the ground."

"Copy. Baggy Zero Four, out."

Just to be sure he was clear of any other air traffic, Rusty dialed in the frequency for Phu Cat airbase, which should be off his right wing in a few minutes. "Phu Cat Control, this is Baggy Zero Four at six thousand, transiting your area."

"Baggy Zero Four, roger, squawk 1200 and Ident."

Rusty hit the correct switch on his radar transponder, and the controller came immediately back, "Baggy Zero Four, radar contact, no traffic. Will advise."

"Thank you, Phu Cat."

Then, against all normal radio protocol, he heard, "Hey Baggy Zero Four, you the same Baggy we worked yesterday?" It was a different voice than the radar controller's.

"Uh, that's affirm. That you, Playboy?"

"Most affirm, little brother. Wanted to let you know we got that revised BDA. You'll never buy a drink at Phu Cat or in the same bar as any Playboy driver, ever." Click click, chimed in the wingman.

Rusty couldn't help grinning. Fighter pilots usually looked down their noses at what they termed "lowly FACs." To be offered free drinks forever – or simply to be called little brother – was a compliment beyond measure. He caught himself daydreaming a bit, remembering the almost hypnotic way that high-drag bombs wobbled their way to the ground. It was almost as though they were seeking a pinpoint target.

And then there was the horrible splash of napalm and the way they…oh crap. He'd allowed the plane to climb. With a start, he saw that he'd gained almost a thousand feet, and he angrily pushed the yoke forward, only to realize with horror that he'd almost pushed into negative G's. Shit, Rusty, he said to himself: you'd better keep your mind engaged or they'll be picking through a pile of shredded aluminum foil to recover the body of that stupid new FAC. Instead of shoving the yoke, he cut the power even more and glided down to six thousand feet again.

A few minutes later, he heard, "Baggy Zero Four, for further flight following, contact Cam Rahn Approach Control, 238.2."

"238.2, roger. Thanks, Phu Cat."

"It was a pleasure, Baggy. We heard about you. Dittoes on the drinks, from the scope dopes."

Damn, even the radar controllers were offering him drinks now!

He contacted Cam Rahn, told them he was inbound, and got a radar vector to the traffic pattern. He wondered if he should tell them about his inability to maneuver much, but decided he didn't want that much attention. They might even call out the crash trucks as a precaution. He didn't want to be that much of a spectacle – or look like a wuss.

Fortunately, he was given what amounted to a straight-in approach. All he had to do was cut the power and he was essentially on a glide path for the runway. By now, his left arm was starting to cramp from the constant pressure he'd been holding. He switched hands and tried to shake out his left arm, but there wasn't enough room in the cockpit to do a good job. He flexed his fingers instead. When he received landing clearance, he switched hands again, set the propeller and engine mixtures, and then lowered the gear and flaps. Nothing to do but drive it to the runway, he thought to himself.

Suddenly, out of the corner of his left eye, he saw a whirling mass of dark green. Snapping his head to that side, he found himself looking almost into the wide eyes of a Huey helicopter pilot. In seconds, they'd collide. Without further thought, Rusty racked the yoke over, slammed the throttles to their stops and pulled back on the yoke – hard. There was a sudden terrible buffeting, a clattering roar, and then a flash of green as the helicopter passed underneath him. Thank God he'd pulled up, and the helicopter pilot had apparently chosen to go down. Or else…

But there was no time for 'or else's'. Rusty felt the O-2 shudder on the edge of a stall. Smoothly and deliberately, he eased the yoke forward again and touched the rudder to level the wings. With the engines screaming, he felt the buffeting of turbulent airflow over his wings lessen and he saw the nose drop down to and then below the horizon. His airspeed crept up a few precious knots. He was flying again. Miraculously, he was almost over the end of the broad runway. All he had to do was bring the nose back up slightly, and he thudded onto the concrete. He bounced once and then settled on for good. Chopping the throttles to idle, he touched the brakes and came to a stop.

"Baggy Zero Four, are you able to taxi?" the tower asked.

"Uh, yeah. I think so. What the heck was that?"

"Army Huey, Baggy. That's all we can say until we review the tapes. You sure you don't need the crash crews?"

"Negative, tower, I'll just taxi to the 21st TASS, I guess." He hadn't noticed the phalanx of red lights and bright yellow trucks hurtling towards him until then; just as he did, they slowed, doused their lights and turned around. He'd made a spectacle of his arrival after all. Calming his heart, he started to taxi in, going through his checklist items. That was when he noticed his G meter: plus 3-something. Oh, shit.

He debated pushing the reset button, but decided against it. The brass would surely get word of his near-midair collision, and they'd seriously question how he managed to avoid it without recording any G's. He left it as is. What he really wanted to see now was that left boom.

As he parked and shut down, he saw the crew chiefs eyes locked on the boom, and he knew. By the time he'd unstrapped and climbed out the right side, there was already a jeep with two majors in it parked next to his plane. Parked on the left side, he noted. They weren't there to give him a ride – unless it was a ride to the brig for damaging a plane.

He ducked under the wing and the rear prop and let himself look. The left boom didn't look bad, at first. Then he noticed the heavy wrinkles in the boom's aluminum skin. He backed up and let his eye align the two booms. The left one had a definite bend in it.

Oh, crap.

"Lieutenant!"

Well, here it comes, Rusty thought to himself. It was a fun flying career while it lasted. "Yes, sir?"

"That was a helluva job of flying, mister. I happened to be watching for your arrival. I cannot understand how you managed to maneuver that violently and not stall out. How the hell do you fly out of a stall that by definition means you are no longer flying?"

"Uh, I beg your pardon, sir?"

"I said…where'd you learn to fly like that? You're one hell of a hot stick. Christ, and in a helicopter's rotor wash, too. Goddamn!"

This time Rusty managed to grin like an idiot, pee his pants, *and* faint.

He came to sitting in the jeep.

"You okay now? You sat down rather suddenly, and you, uh…may need a clean flight suit." The ebullient major was now his nurse.

"Uh, no. No sir. It must have been the heat or the air or something. I got a bit light in the head. I'm fine." He felt the warm wetness. "Uh, I might like to change, though. My bag is…"

"Don't give it a thought, uh, Naille. The chief will get it out for you. We'll head for the TASS and you can change there. Then we'll start on the paperwork for this thing." He jerked his thumb at the plane.

"Paperwork, sir?"

"Oh, not much. Just to start the condemnation process."

"Sorry, sir, I'm still not reading you."

"Oh, of course. Well then…you brought that plane in here on a conditional Red X: technically unflyable. Now it's in even worse shape. We'll condemn it."

"It can't be fixed?"

"Maybe it could be, but believe me, it's much easier to get a whole new O-2 than a major part of one. Besides, this one can be cannibalized for almost all its parts. That's a win-win. Hell we should thank you for putting the poor thing out of its misery. We owe you. What can I do for you as repayment?"

"Uh, a new fluorescent light fixture would be nice."

"A fluores…" The major stared hard into Rusty's eyes. "Are you positive you're all right?"

CHAPTER FOUR

Gomez slipped the chocks into place, then pulled open Rusty's door. "Ay Chihuahua! This one a Cadillac. She even smell like new!"

"She's all yours, Gomez. I traded the old one in. Does this beat the drink I owe you? How you like her?"

"Magnifico!" He backed away, taking in the pristine markings, the gleaming, waxed grey and white paint. He ran his hands over the tires, which were so new they still had rubber whiskers. "Magnifico!"

Whitworth and Blake looked on, both smiling like cats. As soon as Rusty finished with the maintenance forms – an extremely thin set of forms, the plane was so new - they slapped Rusty on the back and peered inside the plane.

"It does still smell new," Whitworth said. "Just like a car on the showroom floor. Unbelievable. Naille, you continue to amaze."

"That's not all, look there," Blake said, pointing to the area behind the front seats. Strapped down with new, bright red cargo straps was a pile of boxes, sparkling new aircraft parts, and two four-tube fluorescent light fixtures. "That's a jackpot!"

"I don't care where you came from, Rusty, or what gods smiled to bring you to us, but I'd kill a goat to keep those gods happy. A veritable herd of goats," said Blake.

"If you saved one for some cabrito, I'd be as happy as two clams, sir," Rusty shot back. "I do love barbecued kid goat." He shot Gomez a thumbs-up, and Gomez nodded enthusiastically.

"If I can ever make that happen, you'll be the very first to know. Promise," Whitworth said, shaking Rusty's hand.

In the hooch, Rusty unveiled two other surprises: a case of genuine Budweiser and a bottle of Tanqueray gin.

"Oh bless you for the beer, Rusty," Brian said, "but why the gin?"

"Well, tonight at Ardmore Hour, when the colonel offers me some of his bottled acetone, I plan to decline because I brought my own."

"Oh brother, will that ever twist his nose! You sure you want to do that?"

"Brian, I am temporarily able to walk on water. I'm not going to waste the chance to exploit it."

"Right on, brother," Crazy Eddie whooped. "Right on!"

Bob, who had been happily rewiring the new fixture into place, yelled out to the porch, "Yeah, yeah. The booze is great. What I want to know is how does a brand spanking new Oscar Deuce fly?"

"Oh, it's a honey, Bob," Rusty said. "Lots of power, it cruises faster than any other bird I've flown, and everything works. Even the seats are comfy. You'll get your turn at it."

"Geez. Tell us again how you managed to snag that plum," Brian said, shaking his head.

"Well, they not only weren't mad at me for severely bending the old sky pig, they were overjoyed. According to them, they can get new planes easier than parts. So they were almost desperate for a mostly good plane to cannibalize. They were licking their chops even before I landed, but couldn't quite manage to write that one off due to a single, non-critical bullet hole. Then an Army Huey nearly ran me down on final, and I managed to bend the boom while evading him. Problem solved from their viewpoint. In reward, they assigned us this new arrival. That's all there is to it."

"Not quite all, from what I heard," smirked Crazy Eddie. "Wasn't there some mention of a wet seat cushion?"

"No, there was not," Rusty said firmly, but choosing not to admit that the wetness came after he'd gotten out.

"Oh lay off, Eddie," Bob said. "What about that damn Huey?"

"I don't know anything about that," Rusty said. "I never saw it until just before we would have hit, and I never saw it again. Never heard a radio call, either. The tower said the radio tapes would be checked, but I didn't hear what they found, if anything."

"Well, I'm sure gonna be a little more careful around here from now on. Those damn 18-year-olds fly like maniacs."

"Bob, that's why the Army hires 18-year-olds to fly choppers. They *are* maniacs. No fear of death, no nerves: all testosterone and no brains. We're not much older, but we're already more mature and more careful. The saw about old versus bold pilots is true," Rusty said.

Light flickered and then steadied in the hooch. "Ta Daaa!," Bob said. "Let there be light. Man, that's much brighter than the old two-tuber. You did good, Rusty."

"We'll see if he still says that at oh-dark-thirty tomorrow when we flick that thing on," Crazy Eddie whispered to Brian.

"I heard that. But since I'm usually the switch flipper, I'll keep my lids closed until I'm ready for the phosphorescent flood of photons."

"Easy for you to say," Crazy Eddie said, lamely.

"Only because you're hogging the Bud. Where's mine?"

"Here's a cold one, Bob," Rusty said. "Hey, what became of the other new light?"

"I installed that one in Whitworth's office."

"Brown nose! No, seriously, that's a good use for it. It was as dark as a cave when I went in there the other day," Rusty said.

"Yup. The Ardmore curse. I think he gave them the rattiest office at his command. Shitty desks, broken chairs and all. Did you see their filing cabinets?"

"No."

"They had to scrounge them. They ended up with the packing crates for mortar rounds. I made them some shelves from rocket boxes. Same thing I used to make our chairs."

"You made these? Damn. You must be a helluva carpenter back home. What do you call those lounge ones again?"

"Those are Adirondack chairs, Rusty. Simple, once you know the pattern. I made lots of them back home."

"Simple for you, maybe. I can't saw a straight line to save my ass."

"You're kidding. That's the easiest thing on earth."

"You'd think so. But I can't do it. Can't do math or music, either. Both of them are like foreign languages to me," Rusty admitted.

"You gotta be shitting me," Brian chimed in. "You can't do music? Or math? And you're a pilot? I don't believe it."

"It's true, though. Oh, I can do addition and multiplication. I can do simple navigation-level math. But you put a logarithm in front of me, and I don't know whether to eat it or burn it in the fireplace."

"Sum bitch. Music either?"

"Nope, the only thing I can play is a radio. And I can't tune that," Rusty said, shrugging.

"Besides flying – which I admit you are fucking good at – what can you do?"

"Write. I am literate," Rusty said.

"Oh, don't tell us that," Bob answered. "I can't even spell. I damn near flunked English in college."

"I majored in English," Rusty said, "Mainly because I can write. I can do a 40-page term paper in one draft – at a sitting. On a topic I've never read."

"Oh, now I have to call bullshit on that. That's not possible," Crazy Eddie said.

"Oh, yes it is. I've done it many times. That's what got me both a degree and a commission, in fact. I started and edited a weekly newsletter in my ROTC detachment in my spare time. I think I still have purple mimeograph ink under my fingernails,' Rusty said, looking closely at them.

"Unbefuckinglievable."

"True, though. Every atom has its place, you know."

Brian stood, Budweiser in hand. "Here's to talents of all kinds. To quarter notes and Cliff Notes. To Shakespeare and Adirondack chairs. To hell and back."

"Hear, hear!"

CHAPTER FIVE

"I know we're busy, but you'll be more use to us after you get to know the area a bit better. So I'm going to schedule you with Bob today," Blake told Rusty. "He's been here long enough that he knows the hottest spots as well as the allegedly friendly ones."

"I thought you showed me all that on our first flight."

"Oh, sure. But I'm a head shed weenie. I can show you the borders of our work area, but that's about it. I almost never get to fly operational missions. And to really learn an area, you need to fly over it almost every day. At almost every time of day, in fact. But Bob will explain all that."

"Head shed weenie? Can a weenie be kosher?" Rusty joshed. He already felt comfortable enough with Blake to treat him as just another guy he happened to be working with, not his direct boss.

"If I'm a weenie, then by rule it's kosher. Frankly speaking," Blake tagged on, deadpan.

Rusty laughed aloud, then Blake did, too. "You know, I eat Hebrew National kosher hot dogs and salami, myself. But I eat them because I want to. Darn good stuff," Rusty said.

"Yes, they are. By the way, I don't try to keep kosher here. I'd likely starve if I did. I guess it's a kind of a...what's the word you Catholics use for an exception to the rules?

"A dispensation? Hey, how'd you know I'm Catholic?"

"I do have your record file, you know."

"Oh, yeah. Of course," Rusty slapped himself on the forehead, comically.

"You're not Polish on top of it, are you?" Blake teased.

"No; even worse. I'm Slovak."

"How is that worse than Polish? Or Jewish?"

"Oh, well. Poles and Jews are only unpopular in some places," Rusty turned deadpan himself. "But no place welcomes an out of town Czech."

Blake stopped dead in his tracks, stared at Rusty for a heartbeat, and then howled in laughter. He guffawed loud enough that two passing Army soldiers stopped and stared at them. He grabbed at Rusty's sleeve. When he finally got himself under control, he could only talk in raspy pants, "Oh…my…God…That is…the…funniest thing…I…ever…heard…I have to…write that…down…Out of…town…Czech!" He laughed some more. Finally, he just motioned to Rusty with a hand, "Go. Go fly."

Rusty walked back to the hooch, where Bob was waiting with the jeep. They piled in and drove down the dusty, downhill road to the flightline. On the way, Rusty asked, "Who's Pilot in Command on this one? Blake didn't say."

Bob shrugged. "Beats me. I don't care, either. Want to flip for it? No, wait. You log it. I have plenty of missions as commander. Besides, I want to see those allegedly golden hands in action."

"Oh, don't do that. I'm no better pilot than you or anyone else."

"I disagree. There's always somebody better than somebody else. In everything: sports, music, flying. There's always a Best and a Worst, and a whole spectrum of talent in between."

"Well, yeah. That may be true, but there's also a giant slug of folks right spang in the middle with almost no differences. That's the bell curve. I'm one of the middies, I think."

"Tain't what the rumor mill says, McGee. Rumor has it you flew that Oscar Ruptured Duck out of what was described as a half snap roll smack onto the runway at Cam Rahn. From virtually no altitude, with the gear and flaps down. And *that*, McGee, takes not just gold but platinum hands."

"Or else pure, blind, 'reach into a sewer and come up with a Rolex' level of luck"

They parked the jeep, did the pre-flight and strapped in; Bob bowing to give Rusty the left – command – seat.

Once airborne, Bob pointed at things on the ground and talked almost non-stop. He pointed out villages and told how many people lived in each one, which hooches were occupied and which not. He told Rusty how many water buffalo belonged in each village. He revealed which day was for market, and which for laundry. He described the pattern of active versus fallow rice paddies, and how big a garden each hooch needed. He pointed out which roads the locals used and when, and how to tell cart tracks from truck tracks. In short, he described the virtually encyclopedic knowledge that an accomplished FAC acquires about his working area – just by looking.

"Remember, any change, and I mean *any* change in these people's lives is significant. And usually suspicious. They always go to market on Tuesday at dawn, but today they didn't? Something kept them from going. Did the VC confiscate their goods? Or is the village being held at gunpoint? Or was the road mined? Or were their carts taken? You see? *Something* happened, or they'd be at the market at dawn on Tuesday."

"I do see. But how do you tell which of those things did happen?"

"You look closer. The village looks empty? Maybe they're all being held inside their hooches. Look at the doorways for guards.

Are VC in the village? Look to see how the ducks and geese are acting – they're better watchdogs than dogs, you know. Carts were taken for cargo? Look in the village where the carts are always parked. And also count the water buffalo. Carts don't pull themselves. Roads mined? Look to see if people are moving on them or not. How far? Walking the edges or driving down the middle? You get it?"

"It's like unraveling a mystery, isn't it?"

"That's a great analogy, Rusty. You put on your Holmes hat and look for the smallest of clues, things that the average person wouldn't even notice. And you assemble those fragments of information into a logical string. Where that string leads is the culprit. In this case, Charley. But the difference between us and Holmes is that we don't call in Scotland Yard; we call in jets with humongous bombs. Then we blow the crap out of everything!"

"I think I'm gonna like that," Rusty said.

"Oh, you will! You will indeed," Bob grinned.

"OK, so we four Baggy FACS work this whole area. Do we all know the whole area as well as you've shown me this one small part of it? I mean..."

"You mean do we all work the whole thing? No. One guy can only have so much area really, really learned. I like to work the villages, but Brian prefers to work roads. Crazy Eddie is a river guy. He knows every frigging ripple in those rivers, and every crossing, and every footbridge, and so on. That's how he found that target you blasted, by tracing truck tracks from the river to a parking place."

"Huh. What's left for me?"

"Any damned thing you like. Like I said, nobody can possibly have this whole huge area down pat, or even a favorite slice of it. Fly some missions looking at everything. You'll soon find some particular aspect that makes your mind click. That'll be your specialty, whatever it is. But you'll also do all the other kinds of missions when you aren't doing Visual Recce. There's patrol support, convoy escort, pink team support and more."

"What the heck is pink team support?"

"Ah," Bob smiled, "Fortunately, it's not being the lookout for gay soldiers in the latrine. Nutso soldiers, maybe, but not homos. No. The Army flies two-helicopter search and destroy missions. They use a little scout helicopter down low – literally *under* the trees sometimes. He's the white bird. Flying cover for him is one or more helo gun ships. They're the red birds. Together, they're pink teams."

"That even sounds dangerous."

"Oh yeah. Big time, especially for the damn little Loach guys."

"Loach?" Rusty interrupted.

"Uh huh. The Army calls them, in it's inimitable style, LOHs. That stands for Light Observation Helicopter, but 'Ell Oh Aitch' just naturally became Loach."

"Ahh, Same as 'Helicopter, Utility' became Huey?"

"You got it. Anyway, the Loaches are called white birds even though they're camo green. They fly those little Hughes 500 helos with short, four-blade rotors. More like turbine hummingbirds. Two-man crews and no arms but their own M-16s. They poke those little things into incredibly tiny holes in the trees, looking for VC. When they find them, it's literally nose-to-nose with them. Kinda like 'Surprise!' and then all hell breaks loose. The Loach pops itself out of the hole, and the gun ships pour rockets and bullets back in. But about half the time, the Loach gets hit or shot down, or they poke their fingers into a bigger hornet's nest than they expected. That's when they scream for air support. And that's why we fly along, above the gun ships, and with tactical air on alert. Some of our hottest air strikes have come from covering pink teams. It's never dull, for sure!"

That evening, after dinner, Rusty quizzed them, "Guys, clue me in here. Bob gave me some great tips today about looking and seeing. But you guys have almost as much time here as he does. So let me ask you, too. What exactly do I look for on a VR mission? I know what they taught us at Hurlburt, but that was Florida and everything was kinda staged. Everything is so different now that I'm here…"

Crazy Eddie slapped him on the shoulder, "Looking for bad guys is a good place to start!"

"Well," Brian said, "You basically look for anything that's suspicious or out of place. You won't see trucks parked in clearings, like on the ranges at Hurlburt. But you might see new tire tracks, or a patch of wilted leaves, or a wisp of smoke coming from the jungle, or footprints through wet grass…stuff like that."

"Or pink elephants," Crazy Eddie grinned.

"You're on a toot tonight, Eddie! Be serious, willya?" Rusty asked.

"I am being serious. Look for pink elephants. The VC use elephants as pack animals, and they turn them out to graze during the day. And elephants like to coat themselves with mud or dust to keep bugs off. Out here, all the dirt is red, so…"

"So the elephants are pink!" Rusty shook his head, astonished. "And any elephants I see are VC elephants, Eddie?"

"Not all. But if you buzz them, not too low and not too aggressively, you can tell. Wild elephants will run at the sound of your engines, but a pack animal is used to engine noise, and won't even lose chewing rhythm. So if they run, they're wild; but if they don't…"

"Then what?"

"You attack them."

"Oh man, I'm not sure I'd want to kill an elephant. I'm a hunter, but that seems wrong, somehow. They are magnificent creatures, and…well…"

"And they may have been the way the VC carted those mortars and rockets in here. The ones that came so close to killing us all the other night, remember?" Bob said.

"Ah. That does put things in a different perspective. I see. I suppose that anything we can do to end this war sooner would also be the best way to protect the innocent wildlife, too."

"Yup, that's the way to look at it," Brian chimed in. "As hard as it might be to get your mind around it."

"OK, pink elephants I understand. What about other stuff?" Rusty went on.

"Before we go on, the same goes for water buffalo as pack animals," Brian answered. "And add in anything else that serves as a cargo carrier: boats, trucks, even bicycles. The VC use them all."

Bob picked up the thread, "And of course, there are signs of encampments where the VC rest during the day. An early morning smoke wisp while they cook the day's rice, trampled grass, new paths, even footprints. A group of people can't help but leave traces of their presence. Remember the destruction a small group of Boy Scouts can leave in the woods?"

"Boy, do I," Rusty said. "But I doubt that trained soldiers who know that being discovered can also get them dead would be as destructive or careless as a troop of ten-year-olds."

"True," Bob admitted. "But they do get careless, nonetheless. Remember, it isn't a weekend camping trip for them. They live in that jungle, and do nothing but carry loads all night every night. Most of the time, they never see the enemy – us – at all. It's got to be a horrible life."

"And through it all, they have to cook, clean, eat, sleep, piss, shit and all. No matter how careful they might be, those daily activities leave traces. You can spot those traces. Well, eventually you can, anyway. It isn't easy," Bob concluded.

Morning came again, and the daily ritual began. Rusty noted that he'd been scheduled in as a full-fledged Baggy. He marveled at how soon it had happened.

"Well guys, I'd better saddle up and get to it," Rusty said. "My takeoff is in 40 minutes. Yours, too, Brian. Shall we share the jeep?"

"You betcha. Let's go."

They pre-flighted and taxied out together. Rusty let Brian take off first, as he had to rendezvous with a truck convoy as overhead escort and Rusty's takeoff time was less critical. Then, with his maps arranged on the empty seat next to him, he got airborne. He climbed to two thousand feet and leveled off at slow cruise speed, then simply started working his way around the edges of their area, flying in a huge counterclockwise circle, the better to see out the left side of the plane.

He flew wide, lazy S turns while he looked at the ground, but saw nothing that looked odd. The tops of the jungle trees were monotonously regular, and the few small clearings seemed pristine. There were no telltale smoke wisps, no footpaths, no truck lanes. Nothing at all that would even hint that a war raged in this land, in fact. The raw beauty of it all struck him. It was exotic beauty to his senses, but beauty nonetheless. The dark green canopy below him was teak and mahogany instead of oak and hickory. The feathery-looking stands weren't willow but bamboo, and the geometrically perfect tree plots were rubber or banana, not apples and pears. But it was beautiful nonetheless. And deadly. If anything alive down there wasn't venomous or carnivorous, it carried an AK-47.

His maps noted unpronounceable place names, but trees and mountains and rivers were much the same everywhere, and the ones below him grew, rose and ran in seemingly untouched splendor. On a whim, he turned and followed one of the many rivers as it twisted through the jungle. The map called it the Song Bai Lap. It ran low and almost clear in this season, but Rusty could see clear scars high on its banks that told of massive floods and churning debris. Huge boulders rose defiantly from the surface in places, and solid beds of rock produced rapids in others. The sun, still low in the east, glistened and flashed off of dew-laden leaves and wavelets on the river alike. It was not ground fire this time, though. The pattern of flashes appeared in a circular, rainbow-hued spot that moved across the ground with him. Everything looked serene, untouched and natural. And then, with a double take, he realized that something wasn't.

It was just a tiny discrepancy; an odd, angular thing. It sat right against the bank of the river, almost covered by overhanging trees. But a corner of something stuck out. A right-angled corner in a scene of smoothly rounded shapes suddenly stuck out like the proverbial sore thumb.

Hey, that's a boat, Rusty thought to himself. A mostly camouflaged boat; and that can only mean one thing, he thought, as he banked and circled for a better look. He made one tight circle, then widened out his path while he plotted the exact spot on his map. When he'd gotten the coordinates down to his satisfaction, he switched his radio to the TOC frequency.

"Baggy Control, Baggy Zero Four."

"Go ahead Four." It was Captain Blake's voice, as he'd expected.

"Uh, I think I have a camouflaged boat tied up here." He passed along the map coordinates. "Please advise."

"Copy, Four. Stand by." Blake answered. There was a tone of anxiety, mild frustration and rushed activity in his voice, even through the electronic mask of the radio.

"Roger, Baggy. It can't be anything else but a boat. It's under an overhang of limbs, but one corner is visible," Rusty added, impatiently.

"Stand *by*, Four." The vocal note was insistent now.

Rusty waited, orbiting a mile or so away but keeping a sandbar and bend in the river in sight to keep oriented. Almost five minutes went by.

"Baggy Zero Four, Control."

"Go ahead, sir."

"Baggy Zero Four, DASC is unable to supply a package now. Report after your mission." Blake said, peremptorily.

Direct Air Support Center? Referring to the DASC meant that Blake had requested an immediate airstrike, but had been turned down by higher headquarters. Unable to supply? What the heck was going on? Rusty dialed in the frequency that Brian would be using with the truck troops. The moment the radio locked in, Rusty understood. The channel was filled with shouting voices, but gunfire and explosions were clear in the background, some apparently very close to one microphone. And he heard Brian reply to that voice with instructions to take cover.

Rusty flipped through the pages of his daily frequency and callsign log. Clearly, Brian was controlling an airstrike against something, and just as clearly, that something had to be a force that was attacking his convoy. But Rusty couldn't find an airborne strike frequency in use – or at least one that was in use by Brian. The airwaves were filled with ongoing airstrikes being run by other FACs, control agencies vectoring planes hither and yon, and excited voices of all kinds. Rusty scanned the sky, but was astonished to realize that he couldn't see another plane anywhere. It was as if he flew alone in a wholly different universe than the swirling air war that he clearly heard in his headphones. High adrenalin conflict and chaos filled one of those worlds, while utter serenity and lush beauty comprised his own. Bizarre; but completely plausible. This is Vietnam, he reminded himself.

On the one radio channel he could hear Brian, Rusty listened avidly to what was happening. It was a one-sided "look" but Rusty could fill in the missing scenes in his mind's eye. Brian was controlling fighters as they wheeled and dove against the enemy, and talking to the convoy commander when he could; getting estimates of where the enemy was, how fierce the attack and from which directions. Then Brian would use that information to re-direct the next attack from the fighters. As he listened, Rusty turned to the southeast. If Brian ran out of marking rockets or gas, somebody would be needed to immediately take over the air strikes. He'd be the logical one to do that, and every mile he could fly to get closer meant a few seconds of time gained should he be needed.

But then, it all seemed to end. The voice of the convoy commander dropped two octaves and slowed to half its former speed. Rusty heard Brian and that voice discuss the situation: the convoy was apparently blocked by disabled vehicles, and would have to stay in place until the wrecked trucks could be towed clear. Some were burning, also, Rusty gathered. And there were wounded to be airlifted out. Rusty waited until all the critical details had been settled, then keyed his microphone, "Baggy Zero Six, Zero Four."

"Yeah, Zero Four. You up this push? I got ya loud and clear."

"You too, Six. You have it in hand? Need me at all?"

"Uh, not now, Four. Had my hands full for a while, though. Where are you, just in case?"

"About fifteen clicks to the northwest of you, I think. I can see smoke on the ground." As he'd started to talk, Rusty had finally picked out a smudge of gray-black smoke through the ever-present blue-grey haze of the humid air.

"Uh huh. That's probably us. I'm at..." Brian gave his position from the nearest TACAN radio navigation site.

Rusty noted his own position from the same site, did a quick mental calculation of the triangle represented by the three points: himself, Brian and the TACAN, then said, "Uh, yup, that seems about right. Do you want me to orbit here, just in case?"

"I think this is over, Four. The bad guys have withdrawn – those that still could, anyway. I don't think they'll be back today. But you might stay on this push, okay? Just in case?"

"I copy all that, Six."

Rusty continued his VR mission for two more hours, seeing nothing but the regular signs of agrarian life below him. Tiny grass-hutted hamlets surrounded by verdant rice paddies, stretches of thick green-black jungle, placid meandering streams, upthrusts of timeless volcanic rock and the distant sweep of sapphire that was the South China Sea filled his eyes; but there was no sign of the enemy that almost surely thronged below him like teeming termites. Again, the bizarre disparity of reality versus appearance struck Rusty.

He landed on time and went to the TOC to debrief with Army Intelligence. It was the same acne-pocked officer who'd sneered at his and Captain Blake's airstrike BDA, of course. Now, he sneered again, refusing to believe Rusty's report of the boat. His uniform pocket bore the name Higgenbotham.

"It had to be a floating tree or something," Higgenbotham said. "We've never seen cargo sampans on that river before. It empties into the South China Sea, and doesn't link to known navigable rivers and supply routes like the Mekong. You were imagining things." He waved his hand dismissively.

"I know what I saw. It's a boat. I saw what I think was the bow. The bottom and sides curved up and inwards to meet it. It was a square bow about three feet wide. The boat was wider than that, but I don't know by how much – or how long it was - because most of it was hidden. But what I saw was no tree. It was man made," Rusty said, emphasizing his point by tapping his index finger on the man's desk twice.

Blake must have overheard the conversation, because he stuck his head into the cubicle behind Rusty. "I believe the Lieutenant. I've already filed his report with my own higher up, and they are considering it for a pre-planned strike. If there's a boat, there may be a storage yard nearby."

"That's a big 'if' if you ask me," Higgenbotham snorted.

"We aren't asking you," Blake said, icily. "We are reporting it to you, as required. There is an enemy cargo craft anchored in that river at that spot at this moment. You may choose to disbelieve what my own trained observer here reports if you choose, but your baseless disbelief does not invalidate the veracity of the report. Furthermore, if the Army is disinclined to confront such enemy activity for whatever reason, the Air Force is not."

"Are you saying that the Army is afraid to engage the enemy?"

"I said nothing of the kind. But if that is the first thought that springs from your alleged mind, perhaps it is also one that has previously arisen there." Blake spun on his heel and disappeared.

Rusty ached his eyebrows. Wow. That threw down a gauntlet! Rusty turned and followed Blake – quickly. Higgenbotham was sputtering like a lit fuse as he did.

Outside, he said to Blake, "Holy smoke. What was that all about?"

"Oh, I probably shouldn't have done that. Especially in front of you. But that little pimply-faced maggot has been a pain in our asses for a long time. He deliberately downplays any intel that a blue-suiter supplies, and pads any that a greenie finds. Once, he even 'accidentally' credited an Army spotter with finding an enemy encampment, when it was actually one of our guys. He apologized when I called him on it, but he smirked when he did – and he never corrected his report, either. He's just a suck-up to Ardmore. And an asshole."

I was right, Rusty thought to himself: there's more than one war going on around here.

That afternoon, neither Brian nor Rusty was scheduled to fly again. They sat in the hooch porch and relaxed. Rusty watched in morbid fascination while Brian scratched and rubbed his bare feet. Greyish-blue patches spread from between his toes and up the arch of both feet.

"What happened this morning, Brian?"

"Oh, pretty much the usual thing for truck convoys: they got ambushed. The VC hits the lead truck to stop them, then hits the last one to box them in. The ground guys scream for help as all hell breaks loose in the middle. That's when the Air Force comes to the rescue."

"It sounds like it's almost rehearsed."

"Well, it is, almost. The details change from time to time, and sometimes nothing happens at all, but in general, convoys attract ambushes like fresh shit attracts flies."

"It almost sounds like the VC know a convoy is coming. Surely they don't sit and watch every road all the time until a convoy happens past."

"Oh, of course the VC know about it," Brian said. "Security is a joke. I'd bet half the locals who work here at Emerald are actually VC, or at least sympathetic to them. They help to load the trucks and such, and before the convoy leaves, the VC know not only how many trucks and when they're leaving, but probably what's on each one, the route they'll take and maybe even the names of everyone going along."

"There are active VC actually working here at Emerald? Why do we allow that?" Rusty asked, incredulously.

"Just stop to think a second and you'll realize what a dumb question that was," Brian laughed. "First of all, how the hell do we tell who's who? The VC don't wear uniforms or carry VC ID cards. If you ask one, do you think he'll admit to being VC? Ask one if another guy is and you think he'll rat the other one out? Would you rat if you knew that you'd be condemning yourself or your own family to death by doing so? Fat chance."

"But wouldn't the good ones turn in the VC ones to help win the war?"

"Rusty, Rusty, Rusty," Brian shook his head. "You clearly haven't yet learned the truth about all this. There is no 'winning' the war for these people. There's only surviving it. They've been at war with somebody or other for generations, maybe for centuries. They've never known anything *but* war. They have no concept of 'after the war' because they have no concept of 'no war'. At all. It's as alien a concept to them as it would be for you to think about living without weather. For you, there's good and bad weather, and there's stormy days and sunny days. But you cannot imagine no weather at all. Neither can they imagine no war."

It was a profound observation, and it stunned Rusty into silence. He stared out of the screened porch for a while, then turned back to Brain. "The logical deduction of what you're saying is that the war doesn't matter. What we're doing here is immaterial?"

"Afraid so, Rusty. Don't take it amiss, but it doesn't. Look, you've seen those little hamlets out there in the jungle, right?"

Rusty nodded.

"Do you imagine that anything, even the smallest detail of their lives, would change no matter who 'wins' this war? That it makes any difference whatever to them if their government is a democracy or communist, a king or a czar?'

"Now that you say it, no. It wouldn't. Well, it probably wouldn't. A Communist government could come in and take their whole food crop, or their daughters, or just kill them all. Isn't that what we're trying to prevent?"

"Uh huh. But so could their current, totally corrupt democratic government. Or a supposedly benevolent dictator. Or just the next hamlet down the trail, for that matter. Which is no change from what they have today or yesterday, or the last century…or the next one."

"Hmmmm. That's a pretty fatalistic and pessimistic outlook, Brian. I wouldn't have guessed it was in you."

"It's also a realistic one. And it *wasn't* in me when I first got here. Just like it isn't in you – yet. But give it time. Give it time. It'll grow on you like this foot fungus."

It was something more akin to cynicism that began growing in Rusty the next day. After breakfast, Blake briefed him. "The DASC is still weighing the possibility of a pre-planned strike on that boat, Rusty, but even you have to admit that it's long gone by now. If you saw it, they certainly saw you, after all."

"Uh huh. I realize that. I just hate to have the Army doubt my word – or my ability."

"I think they put more faith in your report than they'd like to show or admit. They've scheduled a hunter/killer helicopter team to patrol that stretch of river today. Purely coincidence of course," Blake rolled his eyes heavenward.

"A pink team? I'd sure like to know what they find," Rusty said.

"And so you shall. By an equal coincidence, you happen to be the only pilot I have available to fly cover for them today. Strange, isn't it?" Blake's eyes twinkled.

"Yeah, it is. Who'da thunk that? Gee," Rusty replied with feigned amazement. "When?"

"First thing this morning. Nobody thinks they'll find a boat still there, but maybe there will be some trace of an encampment or maybe even some supplies the VC couldn't get away in time. Who knows?"

"I think we all might know before too long. I think there'll be more there than met my eye."

"I do too, Rusty. I can only hope that it'll be as big a find as Eddie had."

"Ouch. I still feel guilty about taking that pre-planned strike out from under him. I owe him one, if this turns out to be more than just some fisherman's rowboat, I'll feel like I've stolen another one from him," Rusty said dolefully.

"Don't give it a thought. Nothing's fair in love or war, they say. This is certainly one or the other," Blake waved his arm to encompass the dreary, blighted camp.

"Well, if this is love, it's suffering under the world's cruelest hoax."

"Then it must be war," Blake grinned. "Why don't you just go wage it to the maximum you are able and let the imaginary scoreboard show what it will. Any 'who owes who' score is in your own mind, anyway. Believe me, Eddie does not keep one."

Rusty shrugged, "I hope not."

Reminding him of his perceived debt to Eddie even more, his plane that day was the new one. Rusty found the pink team as it proceeded southwest towards the river, and he checked in with the team on his radio. Red Hat 22 and 23 were the lumbering gun ships, while White Hat 21 was the tiny scout helicopter buzzing along right on the treetops. Weaving back and forth above them – the O-2 was no race plane but it certainly outpaced overloaded Hueys – Rusty watched the almost hypnotic dance of the gunship helicopter rotors. The top of one blade on each gunship was painted white for easy visibility from above, and the vertiginous result was like watching a boomerang as it looped along in flight. Contrarily, the tiny Loach ship had a four-bladed rotor that spun so rapidly it was invisible, and none of the four was painted. Tracking that tiny, dark green, egg-shaped craft as it darted about right against the dark green jungle was almost impossible. Naturally, visually tracking the Loach was the
94

whole point of the exercise. Army intelligence: the world's greatest oxymoron, Rusty mused.

The actual search for bad guys started well downstream of where Rusty saw the boat. Fascinated, Rusty watched as the busy Loach poked and probed its way not only into the tiniest possible clearings, but seemingly under the very trees themselves. Skimming the water like a hummingbird, it would duck under overhanging tree limbs, disappearing from sight as it hovered around underneath. All the while, the Loach observer carried on a running commentary to the gunships: "Two One is moving west. No contact. Two One is probing this clearing. No contact. Two One is moving to the next opening in the cover. Transiting west. No contact." And so on.

The orbiting gun ships constantly positioned themselves so that one or the other was in position to instantly roll in to deliver rocket or machine gun fire. They seldom broke radio silence, except to reassure the Loach that they still had visual contact: "Two Two has a tally."

All the while, Rusty wove a pattern high above the two gun ships, never speaking on the radio at all, but mesmerized by the calm deliberation of the Loach pilots. What they did really was like reaching your bare hand into a hornet's nest. For his part, Rusty was sweating with anxiety and foreboding.

This aerial dance continued for the better part of an hour with absolutely no enemy contact whatsoever. It was as if the VC had never visited this river. Rusty was beginning to doubt his own sighting, when he looked ahead and saw the long sandbar in the middle of the river. It was right about there where he had seen the boat – or thought he did.

The Loach ducked under the overhanging limbs along the bank again and again, inching ever closer to that spot. The gun ships circled warily. If there were any enemy down there, they'd have heard the sharp WHOP WHOP of the Huey gunships rotors coming for a long time, Rusty knew. They were either long gone or really, really ready for them.

It was the latter.

"Two One is probing the..CONTACT! CONTACT! Heavy fire! We're hit! RPG! Shit shit SHIT!"

Out from under the limbs shot the Loach, but now it was smoking badly. Even from high up, Rusty could see that the entire Plexiglas dome in front of the crew had been shattered. Heavy and ominous black smoke poured from the whole fuselage, and now bright sparks were showering out of the engine area, where the powerful rocket-propelled grenade had hit.

Simultaneously, Rusty heard, "Two Two is rolling in...rockets" and "Two One is going down!"

From above, the gunship nosed over and almost instantly began pouring rocket after rocket into the shoreline of the river. Gray-brown smoke marked where the high-explosive rockets were slamming into the trees, but Rusty's eyes were glued to the Loach. It made a wide right-hand turn, wavering and wobbling drunkenly as it did. Rusty held his breath as it dipped down almost to the surface of the river, but somehow managed to stay airborne long enough to make it to the sandbar. But it wasn't a landing; it was an impact. The doomed craft hit the soft ochre sand almost sideways. Its left skid dug in and with a terrible smack of sand and flying metal, the rotors disintegrated as the craft tipped over. Nothing came out of what was left except ugly smoke for a few seconds, and then Rusty saw one green flight-suited figure dragging another out of the wreckage. The two were only a few yards away when a bright flame whooshed into life enveloping the dead Loach. The two men plopped down into a hole scooped out from under a huge fallen tree's root ball. It was a natural foxhole that protected them from gunfire.

Rusty snapped out of his trance. He flipped the radio selector and stabbed the mic button. "Baggy Control, Baggy Zero Four, a copter's down. Crewman wounded. Need emergency air support. Over."

"Baggy Zero Four, understand you have a helicopter down and crew wounded. We copy this is a rescue. Say your position."

"Uh," Rusty fumbled, trying to collect his wits. He stared uncomprehendingly at his instruments for a second. Then suddenly, his training took over and his mind snapped into complete clarity. "Zero Four is on the 312 radial of Channel 81, DME is 45 miles. Gunships both engaged with enemy forces. I can see multiple sources of enemy fire, on both banks of the river. The scout helicopter is downed and burning on a sandbar midstream. Two survivors, one wounded."

"Copy Zero Four. Alert fighters scrambling, and we are requesting mission diverts from DASC. Hang on." Blake said deliberately, trying to keep Rusty calm.

"Roger, Baggy Control. I copy," Rusty replied in equally measured tones. "Ready to copy fighter numbers when available. I am situation commander as of now." It sounded presumptuous but reassuring, even to Rusty. He switched back to the gunship frequency. "Red Hat, this is Baggy Zero Four. I copy all and have air support enroute. I will direct all air action from now on. Say your status and fuel."

At first, the gun ship pilot audibly bristled, "Baggy, I am the lead cover ship and I have things under control." There was a pause, and then he resumed in a different tone." "Uh, I am running low on ammo and fuel. So is my other. Understand you have assets enroute?"

"Affirmative, Red Hat. Fighters and Dustoff notified." He fibbed about the air ambulance, but needed to take firm control now.

"Ah, copy, Baggy. All right, you have command. I have to break off soon to rearm and refuel."

"How long can you keep station, Red Hat?"

"Um, I think we can each make two more passes with rockets, and maybe one more with gun. Call it ten minutes."

"Okay, Red Hat. I copy. Help is on the way."

A third voice came up, this time on the emergency channel, or Guard. "Red Hat, this is White Hat Two One...Bravo. We're taking small arms fire from both banks down here. Alpha is wounded bad. Get us out of here!" It was the Loach observer talking on his survival vest radio. Two One Alpha was the wounded pilot.

Before he could answer the Loach observer, yet another voice blasted his headset, "Calling on Guard, this is Crown. Say again." Crown was a communications plane, primed and ready to assist in any emergency. A series of Crown birds orbited high over Vietnam 24 hours a day with extremely powerful radios.

Rusty flipped to Guard, "Crown this is Baggy Zero Four. I am on-scene command for a chopper down. Crew wounded. Request immediate air. TACAN 81, 312 at 45. Over."

"Baggy Zero Four, Crown copies. Assets to come. Say your aircraft type."

"Baggy Zero Four is an Oscar Two." That told Crown not only what he was flying, but that he was a FAC – and presumably capable of handling anything.

"Roger that, Baggy. Break. All aircraft, this is Crown declaring an air rescue emergency. Repeat, this is Crown on Guard declaring an air rescue emergency. Any suitable strike aircraft near TACAN 81, report."

Immediately, three or four sets of fighters tried to volunteer their bomb loads to the rescue effort. Rescue of a downed US crew was something that everybody wanted to help with. Crown asked Rusty what he needed. Page after page of weapons characteristics magically seemed to scroll through Rusty's brain, as the long hours of memorization work at Hurlburt bore fruit. His downed airmen were only a hundred yards or so from the enemy but well dug in. They were safe from the bad guys – but lots of air-dropped weapons could prove fatal to them. He mentally winnowed the list of possible weapons down to a few that might be usable.

"Uh Crown, I cannot use slick bombs. I'll need high drags no larger than Mark 82s. No CBU. Guns and rockets are good. Maybe nape. This is a close engagement." He looked down at the sandbar. The wind was light, but blowing across the river from south to north. He might possibly be able to use napalm on the north shore because the wind would blow it away from his survivors. But any less-than-perfect drop on the south shore would fry his chopper guys.

"Crown copies all." Crown began to accept or refuse the offers of several sets of fighters. Meanwhile, Rusty heard Blake talking on the VHF radio, "Baggy Zero Four, Control. You have alert fighters enroute. Blade One One. Estimate arrival in two minutes. Switch to 235.6. Report back on company Victor."

Rusty replied, "Copy fighter info and push. Report on VHF. Did you copy Crown is assisting?"

"Affirmative. You have the whole world up. Gunships cranking now, artillery on standby and Dustoff is enroute."

Thank goodness Blake had called for Dustoff medevac, Rusty thought. Now if he could just manage the mushrooming level of activity that he'd created…

"Baggy Zero Four, Blade One One climbing through one five, ten miles southeast your fix."

Rusty acknowledged the call on his UHF, and started writing on his cockpit window.

"Blade is two Huns, wall to wall snake and nape plus guns. Have you in sight. Ready for brief."

Rusty briefed them about the situation in extreme FAC to fighter shorthand. He flipped back to FM, "Red Hat, break off. Repeat, break off. Fast movers overhead. Exit immediately to southeast, down the valley." Back to Guard, "Crown, Baggy Zero Four on Guard: alert fighters on station. Hold all others above two zero thousand, stacked." Flip to UHF. "Blade, say when ready for a mark. I want snake only on the south bank, nape only on the north.

Make all runs east to west. Friendlies are on the sandbank at midstream. Acknowledge friendlies."

"Baggy, Blade lead is ready for your mark. Acknowledge friendlies on sandbank midstream. Copy snake on south and nape on north banks. Two?" "Two acknowledges and copies."

Rusty nodded to himself. Let's get the show started. He snapped into a rolling dive and launched his first smoke rocket onto the south bank, abreast of the huddled chopper guys. "Lead hit my smoke. Two, I will mark for your first pass also."

"Lead is in with a pair of snakes, FAC in sight."

"Tally on Lead, Cleared hot." Rusty twisted his neck almost out of joint to see, but found Lead flashing down out of the morning sun, perfectly in position. Rusty was turning back over the river, aligning himself to see Lead's drop and then immediately mark for the wingman. The south bank erupted in a spout of green foliage, black smoke and gray mud. WHUMPUMP the twin explosions thumped into Rusty's plane. Without a pause, Rusty bunted his nose over and fired a smoke rocket into the north bank, well back from the edge of the water. "Good hit Lead, Two put your nape no closer than 100 meters from the river at my smoke. Tally on you, and cleared hot."

"Two's in hot. Copy."

Rusty felt the fireball's energy through his own windows as he wheeled again for Lead's next pass. As he did, he heard the Loach observer again on his vest radio, "Shit hot! Hit 'em again!"

"Lead, hit 100 meters east of your last. Cleared hot."

"Lead's in."

Two more thunderous explosions rocked Rusty's plane, then a third. Something on the ground had gone off big time. There must be enemy stuff stored there after all. He was smiling to himself when he realized he couldn't see the wingman. Frantically swiveling his head,

Rusty saw him, almost too late. "Two, abort! Go dry, go dry! Acknowledge"

"Two is off dry."

The wingman had aligned himself so that his napalm pass would cross over the river diagonally from south to north. A drop only milliseconds too early would have put his napalm right on top of the chopper survivors. "Blade flight, make ALL passes due west from the east. Do you copy?"

"Blade Lead acknowledges east to west only."

"Two" came the call from the wingman - sheepish at his grave error. Rusty knew the man would catch hell later, but he had no time to think about that now.

"Okay, Blade Lead hold high. Two, I'll make another mark." As the F-100s maneuvered, Rusty did also, placing his rocket with extra care a good 100 meters away from the river. "Okay Two, hit my smoke. In sight." This time, the gaping, mouth-like front intake of the F-100 lined up perfectly with the river as the plane dropped down from altitude. "Cleared hot."

The silver cylinders tumbled down and split exactly atop Rusty's billowing smoke mark. Concentrated hellfire spewed out with a gush. Anybody under those trees would either have all the air sucked out of his lungs or he'd be instantly incinerated – or both.

After a final bomb pass by both planes, Rusty had them expend all their cannon shells right along the riverbanks. Strafing was extremely precise, and he wanted to use it on the final pass, in case the bombs had driven any surviving enemy soldiers to seek cover right down on the water's edge. He didn't see any VC, but he had the fighters strafe the banks anyway. As the jets zoomed off, Rusty flew right down the river at low altitude. He wanted to look for muzzle flashes on either bank, and he saw none. He set his radio to Guard.

"White Hat Bravo, this is Baggy on Guard. How you guys doing?" It was not proper radio protocol, but Rusty didn't think the two guys down there would mind.

"Hey Baggy, that was awesome. No more enemy fire for now. Can you get us out of here?"

Before he could reply, he heard on another receiver, "Baggy, this is Dustoff. I'm holding south, and see your position. Ready to come in whenever you're ready for us."

"Uh, I copy, Dustoff. Better make your approach east to west, up the river. There may be bad guys where you are. Go ahead and make an approach. Survivor reports no enemy fire for now." Then he flipped back to Guard. "White Hat, stand by for Dustoff...Break. Crown, do you copy?"

"Crown copies on Guard. Standing by. All aircraft responding, maintain silence and stand by."

Rusty watched the unarmed Huey with the red and white crosses on its side dash right up the river at almost no altitude, then pitch its nose up, slowing instantly to a hover. It touched down almost before the sand could boil up around it. He saw a paramedic jump out and sprint to where the two downed Loach men crouched, and then saw one man being carried between the other two. They'd almost made it back to the Dustoff bird when Rusty saw scattered white flashes erupt from the banks again.

"Dustoff is taking fire," the pilot of the supposedly protected rescue chopper said, almost casually. In seconds, the three men clambered clumsily aboard, and the Huey fairly sprung into flight. It skimmed the water for a hundred yards, gaining speed, then pirouetted up into a curving climb to safety.

"Got 'em both, Baggy," the Dustoff pilot transmitted, as cool as if he'd said the cat had gone out.

Christ, those guys have cajones like cocoanuts, Rusty thought. "Crown, this is Baggy Zero Four on Guard. Rescue complete. Repeat, rescue complete."

"Baggy, roger, Crown copies. Do you still need air?" Meaning more fighters, Rusty knew.

"Affirmative, Crown, but I'll handle it off Guard."

"Crown copies. Crown is standing down. Good work, Baggy."

Rusty clicked his mic button twice to acknowledge the compliment, but he was still busy. He flipped back to his VHF. "Baggy Control, Baggy Zero Four. Dustoff on the way with both survivors aboard. I intend to continue strikes here with air assets. Secondary explosions seen and enemy fire still occurring. Pass along request to DASC."

"Zero Four, copy survivors enroute. Good job! Will pass along strike request. Stand by for approval and numbers."

Now that there was no danger to friendlies, Rusty could use almost any weapons that fighters carried. And he did. Because they'd been diverted from pre-planned attacks to help with the rescue, the fighters stacked up above him in holding patterns would no longer have enough gas to return to their original missions. So the DASC "gave" them to Rusty. It was a FACs dream come true: all the fighters he cared to work, a lively and apparently lucrative enemy target, and plenty of marking rockets and fuel. He almost whistled as he worked. By the time he'd exhausted all the fighters and his marking rockets, his side window was almost opaque with grease pencil. On the short flight back to LZ Emerald, he transcribed as much of it as he could still read onto his leg board, and called in a summary BDA report to the DASC. He'd seen several ground explosions from enemy stores, the jungle blazed in three places from what had to be fuel supplies, and he could happily report superb accuracy on the part of every fighter pilot. He magnanimously neglected to mention the one dangerous pass by Blade Two. Besides, he knew that Blade Lead would handle that quietly, pilot to pilot. The jungle was too thick to see many enemy casualties, but there had to be some in there, so Rusty estimated 50 KBA or Killed By Air. It was a guess, but it was probably low, he reasoned.

Higgenbotham sat in his cubicle, fuming. Rusty walked in, soaked to the skin in sweat, red marks still impressed into his face from the heavy combat helmet – and Blake silently trailing behind. Rusty handed him the three-page mission report and BDA without uttering a word. He watched Higgenbotham's red face go pale. Higgenbotham scraped his chair back and marched out and down the corridor to the colonel's office. This time, Rusty was not summoned into that august presence. He and Blake just grinned at each other.

Finally, after several minutes of dead silence in the TOC, Blake said, "Why don't you go get cleaned up? I think you've done enough for one day. In more ways than one."

All three other FACs were sitting on the porch, trying to look casual. When Rusty came in, Brian looked up and said, "Warming up outside?"

"A bit," Rusty said, "But not as much as it is in there." He hooked a thumb towards the colonel's end of the TOC. All four howled with laughter.

When their guffaws finally wound down, Crazy Eddie said, "So - what the heck happened out there? I was airborne and got recalled to ground ASAP. Was told to refuel, rearm and sit on cockpit alert for immediate launch. Then we all heard something about a chopper down, and Superman saving the day. Or something."

Rusty couldn't laugh any more, so he just nodded. "Yeah. Something like that." He slumped into a chair, accepted a cold beer from Bob and went on. "The pink team Loach got shot down in flames – right where I was told I hadn't seen a boat tied up." He grinned, as did all of them, and then went on, "And after that it turned into a real goat rope. I had fighters from here to Zanzibar all clambering to get in on a rescue. I had Crown trying to throw even more fighters at me. I had both our own TOC and DASC sending me gunships, Dustoff and I don't know what else. I think, at one point,

104

they may have been moving the battleship Missouri in closer to shore to bombard the place. But the first guys to make it there were the two Blade strip alert Huns from Phu Cat. They ran some snake and nape, and strafed. Instant quiet from the bad guys until Dustoff got on the ground, and then a few hardy types starting shooting at us again. But the Dustoff crew got both the Loach guys aboard, and they dee dee maued right now." Rusty smiled, remembering how Blake had used that phrase. "Anyhow, I then had fighters to burn, so I did. Blew the whole fricking area to smithereens. No more boats there now. Hell, no more nothing there now."

"How many flights did you work?" Bob wanted to know.

"Six more sets after the first pair. Phantoms, A-7s, more Huns, and even a final set of Vietnamese A-1s. I haven't a clue where *they* came from; they arrived last but hopping like jackals to have at whatever the lions had left. You guys ever work Vietnamese A-1s? Man, those guys are good. If you let 'em drop bombs in pairs you waste one, because the first one goes exactly where you want. I targeted a guy – one last hard-core VC guy – who was shooting at me from behind a palm tree. That A-1 lead pilot just rolled in and casually put two 500-pounders down. One on either side of the trunk, so help me. There wasn't anything left there to get a body count, but I don't think that VC got away!" Rusty realized he was almost babbling, and closed his mouth.

The others stared at him. Crazy Eddie broke the silence. "Shit hot."

"Vietnamese A-1s, huh? Yeah, they're good. You would be too, if you had flown three or four combat missions a day for about ten years," Crazy Eddie said.

Bob and Brian nodded in solemn acknowledgement.

The only sad note to the affair came a few days later when Blake told Rusty the Loach pilot had lost his left leg due to his wounds. Rusty's shoulders slumped.

"Don't let that bother you, Rusty. He's already on his way back to the world, and he went home alive, thanks to you. By the way, the observer recommended you for a medal, but since it has to have the colonel's approval before it can go up through the Army chain, I wouldn't count on it. If it matters, I think you deserve one. You're officially a hero in my book, son."

"What matters to me is that you think so, sir," Rusty said, his eyes misting over.

In his bunk that night, Rusty watched as the moonlight streamed in through the porch screens. A hero, he thought. I'm a hero. A no-shit hero. Funny how I don't feel any different. He recalled the films he'd seen during ROTC classes in which medal winners were interviewed. To a man, they all said that they didn't feel special. They'd just done their jobs. At the time, Rusty thought they were simply being overly modest. Now he knew they weren't. Hell, I was only doing *my* job, he realized. Things just happen, and when they're over, somebody wants to give you a medal.

Weird.

CHAPTER SIX

Things dragged on for weeks after that. Nothing spectacular happened to Rusty or the others. The nightly martini call went back to the usual routine where the Army guys ignored the blue-suiters. Colonel Ardmore and Major Whitworth still addressed each other with cold courtesy. Summer baked on in liquid heat. Even the enemy seemed to take a breather. Or perhaps they simply were rebuilding after two severe losses, both due (hopefully unknown to the VC) to Rusty.

The war raged on in full fury elsewhere, according to Stars and Stripes, the official military newspaper. If you could call it a "news" paper when the only things in it were glowing and cornily written reports of good guy successes. Just the opposite of the newspapers Brian's wife mailed to him in her regular "care" packages. She used the pages of their hometown paper as packing material for her cookies and jars of jam, never knowing that the packing paper was the most treasured of the box's contents. Brian never had the heart to tell her that her cookies always arrived crumbled to dust, or that the jam was somehow always moldy when it arrived. How mold could get into a sealed jar was a mystery, but…well, this was Vietnam.

At any rate, it was the newspapers that Brian carefully unrolled, smoothed and devoured, then passed along to the others. The obituaries, reports of car wrecks and high school dances didn't interest the others as much as they did Brian, but the national news and sports sections received prompt attention from all of them.

Rusty didn't care for sports, but news about anti-war demonstrations, Congressional debates about the war, and denouements by foreign diplomats always captured his attention and raised his cynicism level. It was a love/hate situation: he loved to read about the war from other viewpoints, but he hated what those views were. What the world seemed to say was that Brian had been right all those weeks ago: what they were doing here – risking their lives for – didn't matter.

Either he was turning into a full-blown cynic, or his morale was quickly going down the four-holer with his daily bowel dump. Or, third option, he said to himself, maybe it's just that I haven't heard from Mary Beth in weeks.

It was true. He hadn't gotten a single letter since shortly after arriving at LZ Emerald. He'd asked about his mail at the Army post office on the camp – and gotten no response other than shrugged shoulders. He'd made inquiries back through the TASS at Cam Rahn. Yes, they had submitted his change of address through military postal channels. Sorry, that's all they could do. He'd written to Mary Beth that he wasn't getting her letters. But there was nothing she could do, either – even assuming she was getting his posts. Not a valid assumption, he told himself.

He was short on razor blades, deodorant, lip balm, handkerchiefs, toothpaste and almost all other toiletry staples. That's almost certainly why his duffel bag had been rifled and those items stolen that first night in country: toiletries were simply unavailable anywhere. The only thing anyone could buy was bar soap, and that came down to a choice of Zest or Dial. Either, he'd already learned, was fine on the body and hair, but Dial was the better alternate toothpaste. In this, 'better' was a decidedly relative term. Either one as toothpaste was nasty, but Zest was *really* nasty. Somewhere, he knew, Mary Beth's care packages were sitting undelivered and moldering, chock full of those precious but wasted toiletry items. Or not, and that was even more depressing.

Finally, he was able to get a MARS call through. Mars stood for the Military Affiliated Radio System, and it was a net of amateur radio operators (hams) who volunteered their time and equipment to serve as radio links between soldiers overseas and families at home. From a military phone to a MARS ham, through one or more intermediary hams, and finally into a stateside telephone network, it was possible although extremely unwieldy to hear a loved one's voice. Duration-limited, badly distorted and with no privacy whatsoever, it sucked; but the chance was as precious as gold. To tell all the intermediate radio operators to switch between send and receive and back again, it was necessary to end every statement with the word "over." Soldiers used to radio protocol had no trouble, but

108

wives and sweethearts sometimes never grasped the concept. Calls went astray rapidly when one or more hams tried to intuit who wanted what, and switched, thereby blocking the conversation altogether.

But Mary Beth caught on quickly. After the first few moments while all the various links were established – and while Rusty danced from foot to foot as his allotted two minutes burned away - he heard her voice. "Hi, honey, oh it's so good to hear your voice. Is everything okay, are you okay? Over" Click, whoosh, roar, click.

Rusty: "I'm fine. But I'm not getting your mail. Do you have my address? Over" Click, whoosh, roar, click.

Mary Beth: "Yes, I do. Your letters are coming in fine. Over" Click, whoosh, roar, click.

Then it occurred to Rusty that she may have an address, but was it the right one?

"Honey, read me the address you're using, please. Over." Click, whoosh, roar, click.

Mary Beth: "I'll have to go and find it. Can you wait? Over?"

A disembodied voice: "Sir, you have 30 seconds left of your two minutes."

Rusty: "No, don't go. There isn't time now. I'll try to call again later. I miss you. God, I miss you so much. I love you. Be careful. Bye for now. I love you. Over."

Mary Beth: "I'm fine. Please, *you* be careful, my darling. Everyone here sends you love. When you get home, I'm going to kiss you all...Over" Click.

The line was dead. Rusty went from misty eyes to an amorous growl as he realized what Mary Beth had said as she signed off. Kiss me all...over? Well!

But he still didn't know if she had his correct address. Damn.

Two days later, in typical Vietnam manner, he did know. A whole bundle of battered and bedraggled letters –no packages, alas– came all at once. He simply stared at the envelopes for a long time. Reverently, one envelope at a time, he inhaled the faint trace of perfume that exuded from them. Then, he took several delicious minutes carefully arranging them by postmark date. Finally, as unable to control himself any more than if he were on the verge of a tremendous orgasm, he opened the first one.

CHAPTER SEVEN

It started with a distant growl of thunder and swept down on them like a charging rhino.

It was still pitch black outside and inside the hooch. But the flashes of constant lightning were like the strobe lights of a disco ballroom, illuminating everything in a staccato, jerky, surreal series of still life vignettes. Bob appeared in a series of stark black and white frames as he moved from his bunk to the doorway. Only his voice came through in something other than flickering visual staccato.

"Jesus H Christ. What the flying fuck is that?"

Crazy Eddie rolled over in his upper bunk and shouted over the roar of the torrent slamming into the corrugated tin roof, "It's the monsoon, you idiot. The weather puke said it was due. He even forecasted it, the fucking dickhead."

All four of them assembled in their underwear and tee shirts in the porch, staring at the deluge in fascination.

"Christ, how long do you think this will go on?" Brian asked to no one in particular.

"For six fucking months, more or less, as you damn well know," Crazy Eddie replied.

"Then we're all fucked," summarized Bob. As senior Baggy FAC, he was, of course, right.

After a few more minutes of silently awed witness to the monsoon's first demonstrations of power, all four FACs retired again to their bunks, only to toss and turn until dawn under the terrible drumming of the rain on their tin roof.

"Fuck," said Bob as gray dawn broke, temporarily resuming their rare descent into obscenity.

"Uh huh," said Crazy Eddie, "Where in the fuck did I stash that rain gear?"

"Beats the fuck outta me," said Bob. "Where's mine?"

"Beats me, too," Brian replied, "But I need to take a dump. Now. And I don't care if I'm wet or dry when I do. Or, I should say, my gut doesn't. My gut doesn't care as long as it happens in the next thirty seconds."

"It's my stomach that's inconsiderate," Rusty added. "It wants to be filled. Monsoon or not. But at least my stomach has more than a 30-second window of opportunity."

"Your stomach is enamored of dried eggs and dried milk?" Crazy Eddie mused. "Then your stomach is as unsophisticated as that frog out there." He pointed.

"I believe that is a toad, not a frog," Rusty said. "Witness its warty skin. But I digress. We are immersed – pardon the term- in a Noah-like flood. Yea, a flood of Biblical proportions. How shall we survive?" He held the back of his right hand to his forehead, melodramatically.

"That's easy, you idiot," Crazy Eddie said. "We march two by two wherever we go." He grabbed Rusty by the arm, entwining his, and strode bravely out into the downpour. In seconds, they were both drenched to the skin. "Now, onward!"

Rusty and Crazy Eddie entered the officers' mess hall in their wetly transparent underwear, to the astonishment and disgust of the Army officers already there, and to the delight of Whitworth and Blake, who – as usual - were present as though they'd been glued to the benches.

"Hear, Hear!" said Blake. "Here's to the only sensible, albeit nutso, pair of pilots in the service of Uncle Sam!" He raised his brown bakelite coffee cup to the ceiling in tribute.

"That goes double for the nutso part," said Whitworth, raising his own.

The sopping wet pair sat down, to the consternation of the mess hall stewards, water streaming from their heads and bodies. "Eggs Benedict," roared Crazy Eddie to the perplexed men.

"And cappuccino with extra cream," echoed Rusty. "Don't forget the Bananas Foster for dessert."

The stewards, both black soldiers unaccustomed to being addressed directly under any circumstances, withdrew in confusion and dismay.

In a few moments, the same stewards timidly delivered the usual unpalatable breakfast dreck: reconstituted dried eggs, reconstituted dried bacon, reconstituted dried milk, reconstituted dried potatoes and reconstituted dried coffee.

"Well, at least we have plenty of water to rehydrate this shit," Crazy Eddie observed.

"But not enough to flush it to perdition," Rusty said.

He was more wrong than he would have guessed. Over the next few hours – and days- the earthen cleft between their hooch and the officers' mess filled with rampaging torrents of rainwater. The four-holer was swept away, rebuilt and swept away again. The rain never, ever stopped. It poured down in buckets. It rebounded off any hard surface it struck. It roared down any inclined surface, including the FAC Shack's sandbagged tin roof, to cascade into every available low spot or defile.

When they could not stand to be enclosed within their hooch another moment, they donned ponchos and drove down to the flightline. Their planes were tied down into absolute immobility, but it wasn't them that they had come to view. It was the runway that piqued their curiosity, and it rewarded them with a sight unsuspected. No longer a runway, per se, it was more lagoon than aerodrome.

"How in the living shit are we supposed to take off from that?" wondered Bob.

"We won't be," Brian confidently said. "At least any time soon, that is."

"Wanna bet?" Crazy Eddie taunted. "Ten bucks says that somebody here will be attempting it before the week is out."

"Oh bullshit, Eddie. You really are crazy. It's Thursday already. Ain't nobody gonna try to fly any time soon," Bob intoned.

"Just put your money where your mouth is, pardner," Eddie answered, suddenly appearing to be not so crazy.

That very afternoon, Captain Blake walked into their hooch, streaming water off of his poncho as he did. "Bad news, guys. I need a volunteer."

Crazy Eddie turned to Bob, "Pay up."

Blake ignored him. "I wouldn't ask, but…"

"Yeah, we know. The needs of the service come first," Brian intoned.

"Well, yes they do, actually," Blake replied. "But this is more human. One of the Army troops here came down with an inflamed appendix last night. If it bursts, he's dead. They haven't the facilities here to operate, and they've asked us to see if we can airlift him out. They can't get a helicopter airborne, either, to answer your nascent question, Bob."

Bob sat there, mouth half open, with that very objection poised on his lips.

There was silence as the four FACs looked at each other from the corners of their eyes. Nobody spoke.

114

Finally, shoulders slumping in capitulation, Rusty said, "Life or death?"

Blake nodded. "More like certain death. Not a pretty one, either."

Rusty thought to himself, Oh sure, twist the knife. But he relented. "OK, I'll try. Damn your eyes."

"Piratic slogans aside, that's damn brave of you, Rusty. Come along, I'll brief you in the jeep. Bring your IFR sheets and maps. The enlisted guys have your new plane ready as soon as you are."

Yup, thought Rusty to himself. He wanted me all along. 'Your new plane' my bleeding ass: I've been shanghaied.

When they got to the flightline, Rusty's pallid passenger had already been strapped into the rear, third seat. He looks like shit, thought Rusty. Half dead already, or more. If there had been a bottle of intravenous stuff hanging from the plane's ceiling, he'd have refused the whole idea, he thought to himself. But there wasn't. Oh, well.

"It's only a few miles to Phu Cat," Blake said as Rusty strapped himself in. "You can't miss it."

"Yeah, right," Rusty said, "Just like that ridge of karst between us and it. I'll be damn lucky to miss that, too."

"Now, don't get funny on me, Rusty. Once you're up, you just have to climb to five grand to clear that ridge. Nothing to it."

"Except for the 'once you're up' part," Rusty replied. "And we both know it should be 'IF you get up' at all."

"Nah. I have every confidence in you," Blake said.

"Then you come along," Rusty said, almost acidly.

"You don't need the weight of a decrepit old has-been sandbag like me," Blake rejoined. He actually smiled when he said it. "Not to say 'dead' weight."

Rusty couldn't help himself. He grinned and shook hands with Blake.

He shut and locked the right-side door. He arranged the maps and charts on his leg board and on the seat next to him. He took a careful look at the very sick guy in the rear seat, and then at the woeful figures of Gomez and Blake standing in the deluge outside, ponchos streaming, watching him. He started the engines.

When he got to the runway, he looked out and saw to his horror that the standing rainwater came almost halfway up his main gear tires. Not only would he not be able to see the potholes in the runway, but the horrendous drag of the water against the tires might well keep him from accelerating enough to get airborne. If that were the case, his passenger needn't worry about his appendix.

Rusty splashed his way to what he judged to be the very utmost end of the runway, then turned into the wind. Luckily, it blew strong and steady. He'd need every extra molecule of air moving across his wings that he could get. Dutifully, he checked the magnetos and propeller controls, set the flaps at one-third for takeoff, closed the engine cooling cowlings, and took one last, deep breath. Standing on the brakes, he shoved the throttles fully forward. When the engines stabilized at their maximum power output, he shrugged resignedly, and popped his toes off the brake tabs. The O-2 did not lunge forward; it wallowed. Almost nothing happened at all. He could almost hear and feel the tires rolling through the muddy gunk: whup…whup…whup..whup..whup.whup.whupwhupwhupwhup…on and on. The white runway edge marker lights lumbered past in agonizing slowness – and every one marked runway behind him and therefore worthless to him.

The airspeed indicator trembled and edged upwards. The engine instruments shuddered in exertion. Water and mud flew from the tires – the only things that might fly tonight, Rusty mused, with fatalistic detachment. At forty knots airspeed, Rusty pulled back on
116

the yoke, hoping that the lessened drag on the front gear tire might make up for the added drag it caused on the wing. Soft field takeoff, they had called it at Hurlburt. Not a maneuver that needed to be practiced, they'd blithely assured him. Right, cursed Rusty to himself. Bastards.

Sixty-five knots, and the plane began to slosh sideways in the muck. The wind, never straight down any runway he'd ever used, was buffeting him, trying to blow him off into the rough boundary. He danced on the rudders, but daintily to avoid the least addition of drag. Drag was his enemy now, not time, not smug Army officers, not even the damned VC. Drag. Three fourths of the runway was behind him now, and he had less than three fourths the needed airspeed. It didn't look good. He eased the nosewheel back down a bit, testing to see if it lessened the drag or not. It didn't seem to matter.

Eighty knots. He needed ten more to yank the plane clear of the grasping, greedy water. Out of the deepening afternoon gloom appeared the sight that he dreaded: the line of red lights that marked the absolute end of the runway. They were too close. But if he hadn't the room to accelerate, he also hadn't the room to stop. One was as bad as the other, he thought, and shoved the throttles so hard that he thought they might bend. From somewhere, from nowhere, a powerful gust of wind hit him. The airspeed surged in that gust, and Rusty reacted on purest instinct. He pulled the yoke back in desperation. The tires leapt free of the sucking water, the wings seemed to grab onto the air as if it were a solid bar of steel – and held on. He felt the plane wallow, almost but not quite flying, as the runway threshold flashed under him. He held his breath, and…nothing else happened.

The engines continued to roar, the feeling of sluggish water skiing ceased, the gray of the deluging rain became less a solid wall than a bubble. They were flying. He dared not so much as breath, though, until the airspeed climbed past ninety. He achieved that in mere moments, then milked the yoke back to hold that magic number. As soon as he had a hundred feet of air beneath him, he reached for the landing gear lever and shoved it to "UP." As always, the O-2 sagged and sank down a bit as the huge landing gear doors opened and the gear retracted to the rear. When they closed and the "gear in transit" light went out, he slapped the wing flap lever up. Only when they had retracted and the airspeed surged upwards, did Rusty dare breathe again. They were safely airborne.

Now he knew why Blake had assigned the new plane to this flight. If this had been one of the others, with tired, old engines…it wasn't a pretty thought.

"Emerald tower, Baggy Zero Four. Airborne and enroute." It was a call he'd never made before. For a moment back there, he thought he'd never make any call ever again. But it was a call he would never forget making.

He turned east, hoping to gain altitude out over the flat terrain between Emerald and the sea. Only when he'd climbed to that magic five thousand feet did he plan to turn southward toward Phu Cat. The hard, grasping talons of cruel volcanic karst wouldn't rip the belly out of his plane. Not today, he hoped. The Phu Cat TACAN beeped its recognition code in his headset, and his navigation needle swung solidly to the south. As soon as he was anywhere near, he'd contact approach control for all the assistance they could provide. Surely they'd have no other traffic to guide on a day like this. Suddenly, he groaned. He'd forgotten to pick up his overnight kit or clean clothes. If he were stuck at Phu Cat for long, he'd soon smell like a dead camel. No, strike the word dead, please. Not a good thought right now.

He dialed in the correct frequency, and called. "Phu Cat Approach, Baggy Zero Four. Thirty miles north at five for landing."

The reply was long in coming. "Uh, Baggy Zero Four? This is Phu Cat Approach. Sir, Phu Cat is closed. Has been for two days. We have water on the runways."

Really? Rusty thought. Gee, it was nice in Hawaii when I left there a few minutes ago. "Phu Cat Approach, Baggy Zero Four has a medical emergency aboard. This flight is an emergency, do you copy? Your hospital is waiting for this patient."

"Baggy Zero Four, stand by."

Jesus Christ and his Mom in a bottle, Rusty swore aloud. What nitwits are these pukes? Can't they get anything straight? How dare they not know I'm coming?

"Baggy Zero Four, our hospital says they know nothing about any medical emergency inbound. What is the nature of your emergency?"

I'm not a damn doctor, Rusty cursed to himself. How the hell do I know? He keyed the mic, "Phu Cat, I'm told the patient has a blown appendix or something. Whatever. It's life threatening. And I'm landing there with him whether you expect him or not. And if I get my hands on you jerks for delaying me, that'll be life threatening, too, but not for him. You copy? Now give me vectors to the damn runway!"

"Um, roger that, Baggy. Turn to one seven five for vectors to runway one niner. We'll have an ambulance waiting. And a crash truck. Squawk Ident."

Gee, thanks. Glad you have so much confidence in me, Rusty thought. "Copy one seven five for one niner. Squawking."

Baggy Zero Four, radar contact. Maintain five thousand. Altimeter is two niner seven eight. Negative traffic," he added as an unnecessary remark.

"Yeah, tally ho on the negative traffic," Rusty returned the dumb joke.

Rusty concentrated hard on his instruments, trying to keep the ride as smooth as he could in the fierce turbulence. But even over the engines and the roar of the rain on the plane's skin, he could hear moans from the back seat. Poor bastard, he thought. I sure hope you make it. 'Cause if you don't, I'll be really pissed.

"Baggy Zero Four, turn right to one nine zero, cleared for the ILS approach to runway one niner. Cleared to descend per the approach. Cleared to land. Hell, cleared to do whatever you want, sir. The field is yours."

Rusty had to chuckle at that. He was lined up with the runway, per the approach controller's directions, and also by the ILS receiver needles he now included in his instrument crosscheck. Outside, all he could see still was a solid bowl-like wall of dark grey. The grey was darker than before, too. Night was falling fast. Just what the doctor ordered, he mused, morbidly.

When the glide slope needle came down from the top of the instrument, Rusty lowered his landing gear and flaps. He set the propeller and mixture levers and let the airspeed decay to ninety knots, then bumped a tad of power to hold it there. Constantly fighting the turbulence, he pulled back an infinitesimal amount of power when the glide slope needle centered over the tiny aiming circle in the center of the ILS instrument. He started down the glide slope. Now it was just a matter of keeping the two needles (lateral and vertical) centered like crosshairs while he held airspeed, and he would theoretically descend right onto the invisible runway. Theoretically. It would help if he could see the thing before he hit it. By rule, he was not to descend below a posted altitude unless and until he did see the runway. But Rusty had no intention of following that silly-ass rule. Not tonight. He'd plant this buggy on something even if he did it completely blind. With any luck, that something would be the runway.

He flew down to the posted minimum altitude, and doubted himself. He could see nothing at all except blinding, pouring rain. He slapped his landing lights off to see if he could see better without their glare. To his relief, he thought he could see lights out there. Vaguely. But were they the white lights that outlined the runway, or the street lights of scenic downtown Phu Cat? Nah, there can't be streetlights in Phu Cat, he almost laughed. He pulled back power, held the nose up, and simply waited for the impact.

It was surprisingly gentle. With a squeak, his main tires hit something that felt like concrete. Rusty jerked the throttles to idle and stood on the brakes. In seconds, he was stopped. Somewhere. "Uh, Phu Cat tower, Baggy Zero Four is landed. I'm on the runway, I think. But I don't know for sure. Send that ambulance out here mach schnell and see if they can find me. I'll leave my lights on for ya." He turned his landing lights back on, and just waited.

"Uh, we copy you down, Baggy Zero Four. Do I understand you cannot see well enough to taxi? After you've landed?"

"That's affirmative, tower. Why?"

"Uh, never mind, Baggy. Hey, are you the same Baggy Zero Four who ran that airstrike with Playboy Two Six a month or two ago? And the same guy who ran that chopper rescue single-handedly?"

"I admit to that, yes."

"Oh, well then; that explains it. The Playboy guys claimed you are the world's greatest living FAC, and a while back, the alert Blade guys said the same thing. So a blind landing on a flooded runway, at dusk, with a medical emergency aboard ought to be duck soup for you. Right?"

Rusty couldn't tell if there was sardonic humor behind that radio-distorted voice. So he played it straight, "Uh, I suppose so. I *did* manage to do precisely that, as you can witness."

"Damned if you didn't Baggy. Yeah, damned if you didn't. I'll be go to hell."

"Don't need to, my friend. You're already there," Rusty replied with the cliché.

When he saw flashing lights and piercing headlights appear out of the pounding rain, he shut down his engines, right where he sat – wherever that was.

Two days later, he taxied in at LZ Emerald, his head swimming and stomach flopping about. He had a world-class hangover and worse. The Playboy guys, the Blade guys and the radar approach guys were all good for their word: Rusty had a fresh drink in his hand, whether he'd been conscious or not, for two days. He stumbled out of the plane and over to Captain Blake, who sat waiting for him in a jeep. Blake squinted one eye and looked Rusty up and down, then leaned close and sniffed at Rusty's breath. "Holy North Sea crude. We could run the shower heater off your breath, son. Are you in any shape to be flying?"

"Nope," Rusty answered, truthfully.

"Well then, it's a good thing you aren't on today's schedule," Blake answered. "Whatcha got in the bag?" He nudged the bulging laundry bag between Rusty's feet.

"Stuff. For the guys," Rusty slurred.

At the hooch, Rusty weaved his way in, bouncing off the screen door and tangling himself up in the bug netting as he collapsed into his bunk. Blake handed Brian the laundry bag.

"What's this?" he said, pretending not to have noticed Rusty's entrance or his condition.

"I don't know. He said it's for you guys, though."

Brian tugged the cords open and peered inside. "Oh my God. It's toothpaste, and razors, and toothbrushes, and foot powder, and…and deodorant, and honest to God shampoo! Tons of the stuff!"

"Hey, how'd that Army dude make out?" Crazy Eddie asked Blake.

"He made it. Of course."

Mercifully, after those horrid first few weeks, the monsoon weather began to improve. For days at a time, there would be patches of sun between the towering rain clouds. Mornings would be almost cool, with fog on the deck and broken clouds above. In the afternoons, thunderstorms would sweep through in their violent parade. But a skilled, careful pilot could fly, and fly they did. Every available moment was spent up looking for fresh signs of enemy activity because, oddly, the wet season was when Charley seemed to move more stuff and bodies than otherwise. Perhaps they felt safer under the low ceilings. Certainly they could tell that bad weather meant no fighters, no Hueys, no FACs - and they made the most of it.

Brian, patrolling his favorite roads, discovered a truck park and destroyed it. Bob patrolled the various little hamlets and managed to puzzle out several where the VC had evicted the proper residents (sometimes with sickening cruelty) and taken them over. Crazy Eddie even started calling them the killer Bs due to their success. Crazy Eddie dogged the rivers like a muskrat, finding hidden fording spots and even an underwater bridge. Rusty did a little of everything. Enemy action came like the monsoons themselves: when it rained, it poured.

Bob Strunk was up on a routine VR mission one morning when Blake came down to the FAC hooch. Rusty and Crazy Eddie were there. "Guys, it's time to go down to the flightline."

Crazy Eddie looked up, "Huh? We don't fly for hours yet. Brian is down there prepping for his mission, but we aren't on the morning schedule. Or are we?"

"Nope, you aren't. But we need to surprise Bob." He pulled a sheet of paper from behind his back. "Bob has orders. He's going home. He doesn't know it, but he's flying his last mission right now."

"YEE Haw! His DEROS? Oh, man! And he doesn't know this is his fini-flight?" Crazy Eddie jumped up from his chair.

"Nope. Let's go wet him down," Blake said, smiling.

Rusty looked from one to the other. "What are you guys talking about?"

Blake knitted his eyebrows. "You mean you don't know what a DEROS is?"

Rusty said, "Well, yeah I do. It's Date of Estimated Return from OverSeas, right? But what's the other stuff?"

"Come on, we'll explain while we jeep down to the flightline," Crazy Eddie said.

When they were on their way, Blake said to Rusty, "You know that the war is winding down and that it's not uncommon for guys to be sent home before their normal full year, right?"

Rusty nodded.

"Well, Bob's tour is over. We got a copy of his DEROS orders this morning as part of the frag order. He leaves here tomorrow for out-processing."

"OK, that's not a major surprise, but why THIS surprise? Why didn't you just tell him about it when you got the word?"

"Because if I'd told him he was almost done, I'd also have to ground him. Yes, I'll explain," Blake said, seeing Rusty about to ask. "It's like this...Way back in World War Two, it was common for guys to get killed on one of their last few missions, with a suspiciously large number dying on their final flight. Well, they did a study of guys who survived, and it seems that on the last few missions – if a guy knows they *are* his last few – a pilot tends to get more cautious. More reluctant to be aggressive might be a better way to say it. And when he does, he hesitates; he hangs back from danger. Make sense?"

"Sure."

"And that's what gets him killed. He's been surviving on his aggressiveness, his courage, his willingness to attack, shoot first, fly
124

hard. Suddenly, he loses that edge because he knows he's so close to going home. And without that edge…he doesn't go home at all."

"Ahh. I see that. So now, you keep it a secret when a guy is leaving?"

"Yup. And especially when it's his last flight. So if Bob had stumbled on something big out there today, he'd be the same aggressive FAC he's been for almost a year. He didn't – or he hasn't yet – but when he lands, he's done. Fini," Blake added.

"I'll be damned."

"Could be," Crazy Eddie said from the back seat. "I'd definitely bet on that."

"Oh, blow it out your ass, Eddie," Rusty said, grinning. "So how are we going to break it to him?"

"With a hose. We'll hide behind the revetment wall, and when he climbs out, we'll leap out and hose him down. Then we'll open this," Blake said, reaching into a bag and pulling out a bottle of champagne.

"Champagne? Honest to God champagne? Where in the living hell did you get that?" Rusty stared incredulously.

"Oh, maybe the same place some other hot-shot around here manages to find shampoo and razors," Blake said wryly.

Crazy Eddie laughed so hard and suddenly that he snorted snot of his nose.

"Hmmm…touché," Rusty said to Blake. "You ain't telling either, huh?"

"Hit my smoke, Rusty. Right on."

They parked the jeep, let Sgt Washington in on the secret and unrolled a fire hose. Before long, they heard Bob's O-2 approach, circle and land, and a few minutes later, taxi in and shut down. Blake peeked slyly around the corner of the steel revetment and waved the others back. Crazy Eddie held the fire hose and giggled in anticipation, until Blake whispered, "He's signing the forms. Wait. Now he's taking off his chute. Washington is putting the forms in the plane. As soon as he closes the door…Ok. NOW!"

They rushed around the corner, whooping and yelling like attacking Apaches. Bob stopped in mid stride and glanced at them quizzically. Then he saw Crazy Eddie with the fire hose, and he bolted like a rabbit. Too late. Eddie yanked back the nozzle handle, unleashing a wide fan of water that narrowed to a narrow stream and caught Bob squarely in the back. The water stream almost knocked him down, spinning him around so that in a microsecond, he was soaked from head to toe.

That's when Bob reversed his field and ran straight at Eddie. He grabbed the hose nozzle. They wrestled for it for a second, water spraying everywhere, but then Bob jerked it free. Grinning wildly, he quickly fanned the stream like a machine gun. He wet down Blake, Rusty, Eddie, Washington and the plane in seconds. Finally, with a yell, he yanked the nozzle control closed and dropped the hose. He grinned at everyone. He knew.

Blake said to him, "Yup. You're going home. You're done here, Bob. Congratulations!" He said it he as he was walking to the jeep, and he pulled out the champagne, twisting off the wire cage and popping the cork in almost one movement. White foamy wine spewed out right onto Bob's chest. "Drink up."

Naturally, he didn't. Bob stuck his thumb over the bottle mouth, shook wildly and sprayed wine over everyone else first. Having completed the silly ritual, he up ended the bottle and drank deeply. As soon as he lowered the bottle, he said, "When?"

"Tomorrow morning. No sense delaying the inevitable, huh?" Blake grinned.

Playing along, Bob feigned a frown, drug one boot toe in the mud and said, "No, I guess not. I'll take my medicine." And immediately, he cackled in glee and up-ended the bottle again.

"Hey, hey, what about us! Save some for me," Crazy Eddie said.

"Yeah, and emphasis on the us part. Go easy on that. You already wasted most of it, you selfish jerk," Rusty said, laughing.

Back at the hooch, they fired up the shower to get the sticky wine off all of them, and Bob started to pack his things.

"Jesus. Home. I can hardly believe it." He looked around the hooch as if he were dreaming. "The world. My God...stores, my car, ice cream...my wife."

"I think it'll be 'not necessarily in that order' but...yeah. Geez. Mini-skirts. Eggs – real eggs. Real milk. Oh man, don't even start." Crazy Eddie moaned, eyes closed. "Oh man, you're killing me."

"Yeah, me too," Rusty said. "God. It really is another world back there, isn't it?"

"It's THE world, Rusty. All this is an illusion. A bad dream," Eddie said.

"A nightmare, you mean," Rusty said. Then, "Hey, no downers. Not today. This is a happy day – for Bob, anyway. Let's celebrate." He went to the fridge and took out beers.

"Uh, maybe we'd better not – not yet anyway. You and I have to fly soon, brother."

"Oh, yeah. I almost forgot. Shit. Oh well," he put the beer back. "Besides, Brian isn't here. But wait until this evening, Bob. You are gonna get a Baggy FAC sendoff for sure. If you step on the freedom bird sober, it won't be our fault."

Bob grinned. "I second that! Plenty of time to sleep it off on the way home." He stopped and stared vacantly again. "Home. Jesus, I can't get over it. Home…" He suddenly teared up, and a drop trickled down his left cheek, then another down his right. "Damn, guys. I'll miss you."

Rusty almost cried right along with him, but managed to avoid it by turning flippant, "Oh bullshit, you won't even think about us once you're flying…Hey, what IS your assignment? What'd you get?"

"Christ, I didn't even look!" Bob dove for the sheet of paper with his orders, scanned down through the official mumbo-jumbo, "uh…"Report to..Hey, it's MAC! A C-141! That's just what I wanted. Holy cow!"

"Where to?" Crazy Eddie asked.

"Scott. MAC Headquarters."

"You're shitting me," Rusty said. "I grew up there! Hell, watching planes in the Scott Air Force Base traffic pattern is what made me want to be a pilot in the first place. Damn. You lucky bastard."

"Is it nice there?" Bob said, already getting eager to start his new life.

"Belleville Illinois? Um, well…I grew up there, and it's really all I knew until I started flight school, but I guess it's okay. I mean, it's a hell of a lot better than Laredo Texas, or Clovis New Mexico. For damn sure."

"Yeah. Clovis. God, what a hellhole that was. Talk about polar opposites to Hurlburt, huh? Crazy Eddie mused.

"No shit. But even Clovis is better than here," Rusty said, trying to lift the tone yet again. "Anywhere in the world is better than here, and you're going to dead center in the world, bud. I think you'll like Illinois."

"Me too. And C-141s. What a change that'll be from the Oscar Duck. Room to stand up; hell, room to take a shit, take a nap and cook a meal on those things! And flying everywhere, getting duty-free stuff…man…" He trailed off, daydreaming.

"You think your wife will like Airlift Command with you being gone a lot?"

"My wife…Oh shit! My wife! Oh man, she doesn't even know I'm coming home. And weeks early to boot! Crap. How can I tell her the good news?"

"From here? No way at all, man," Crazy Eddie said, shaking his head. "You'd beat a letter there. Maybe you can send a telegram from Cam Rahn. But other than that…" He slapped himself on the forehead, "Oh man, talk about culture shock. Hell, you can phone her when you land in California, man! They have phones in the world!"

The three stared dumbly at each other, stunned for a heartbeat, then laughed themselves into pain. Phones. They'd forgotten that phones even exist.

That evening, they emptied the fridge, toasting Bob again and again with the last Carling Black Label beer he'd ever voluntarily drink again. With the promised results: Bob was half smashed and half hung over when they stuffed his bag and him into an O-2 the next morning. Major Whitworth sat in the left seat for the flight, headed for an area ALO meeting after he dropped Bob off at Cam Rahn. They popped a dozen smoke grenades at the runway edge as Whitworth roared by them on takeoff, Bob leering down at them from the right-side window. And then Bob Strunk, Baggy Zero Three, was gone.

It hit him more than he thought it would. Rusty stared at Bob's empty bunk the next day and said to nobody in particular, "Damn. He's really gone."

Crazy Eddie rolled over in his own bunk and propped up on one elbow, "Uh huh. You better get used to it. Brian and I will be next, you know. I'm a short-timer, and he's a two-digit midget."

"Brian has less than a hundred days to go? Damn, with everything cutting back and all, he could go any time."

"Uh huh. That's what I mean. I heard they're gonna close Cam Rahn."

"What? Where'd you hear that? Cam Rahn? No fucking way. It's one of out biggest bases in Nam! It's not just an air base, it's a major port and all, too. Nah, that's a bogus rumor. Gotta be."

"Don't think so, bro. I have it from a reliable source. Cam Rahn is as good as gone the way of the white buffalo."

"Who told you? Blake? Whitworth?"

"Nope, better: the desk clerk at 21st TASS Admin. If anybody knows shit like that, it's a two-striper admin puke."

"Yeah, that's sure true. Damn. Cam Rahn closing? That's like the beginning of the end, man. This war is as good as over."

"Yup. And that's not the only place closing, either"

"Where else?"

Crazy Eddie didn't speak, he just pointed at the floor.

"You're shitting me. Here? When?"

"I don't know for sure. But soon. Soon enough that we might not even get a replacement for Bob. No point in it, I guess."

"Damn. Double damn. The end of the war...wow" Rusty mused, dazed by the concept. "Who won?" He meant it as a joke, but it somehow didn't sound like one.

"Well, who's leaving Vietnam and who's staying?" Crazy Eddie raised his eyebrows. "Us and the gomers, respectively. There's your answer."

130

"Triple damn. I can't believe we lost to a bunch of gomers dressed in black pajamas."

"We didn't lose it, brother. We gave it away. Well, not us; not the FACs, or the Air Force or the Army. Not even the South Vietnamese Army. The politicians gave it away. Ours and theirs. Just fucking gave it away. That moron Johnson, mostly; him and that absolute prick MacNamara. Tied our hands, blindfolded us, took away our best weapons and then said, 'Sic 'em – but don't hurt 'em'. Christ."

"I said it before and I'll say it again, Eddie: you ain't crazy after all."

"Hmmm. Don't let that get out, okay?" He grinned, the white of his eyes and teeth glowing down from the gloom of the upper bunk like Alice's Cheshire cat.

"Listen, while we're alone, there's something I have to ask," Rusty said.

"Sure, shoot, " Eddie said, shrugging.

"Before the monsoon, I must've seen you sunbathing damn near every day. Naked. And you were still dead white all over. Except for your hair, of course. What the hell explains that?"

"I just like to be naked."

"No, I mean the whiteness, you idiot. Despite all that sunbathing, I mean."

Eddie shrugged. "Oh all right. You want the real answer?"

"YES! I do!"

Eddie smiled mischievously again, "Beats me. I just never tan. The sun feels good, and I soak it up like a lizard. Never even burn."

"Not even your, uh…"

"Nope, not even them," He laughed. "Haven't a clue why not, though. Just chalk it up to Vietnam. This whole place is bass-ackwards and up-fucked."

Rusty just nodded. Yes, it certainly is.

CHAPTER EIGHT

"Rusty, I'd like you to take over a mission that Bob used to fly," Blake said to him the next day. He led Rusty down one of the numerous paths of white painted rocks that crisscrossed LZ Emerald.

"These aren't primroses, are they?"

"What?"

"Never mind. What mission?"

"Oh, the rocks. Cute. No, it's patrol escort. You know that the Army runs long-range patrols out of Emerald, right?

"Yeah: long, short, whatever. They run all kinds of patrols, all the time."

"Well, these are a bit different. Not just longer. They're actually a kind of Special Operations mission. Very covert. The teams go out for not just a few hours, like you've worked already. These guys are gone for days or even weeks. And they're not just Army; they're Rangers."

"Oh ho. I see. You mean cloak and dagger stuff?"

"Well, the short answer would be 'yes' but it's complicated."

"You astound me," Rusty deadpanned.

Blake rolled his eyes. "All right, I know. What isn't. But on these missions, you'll be flying with a right-seater. He's the team's communicator. Your job, basically, is to get the right-seater to the team's general area, and he talks to them. Then you bring the right-seater home."

"I'm a taxi driver? Gee, you're right. This IS complicated."

"You get more cynical by the day, Rusty. That worries me. But that aside, your role can be a lot more vital. The team's often go 'hot' and then they need to be exfiltrated before they get compromised."

Compromised? What does that mean?"

"It means that some of the teams go…let's just say, outside the normal bounds of…"

"Vietnam," Rusty finished for him. They go...does it start with a C?"

"And L."

"Ahh. It figures. Cripes, that's a long way from here."

"They are called long range…"

"Uh huh. I get it. They leave from here?"

"It's more deniable that way."

"I bet. It's fricking nuts, so it must be true. Don't tell me the poor bastards walk all the way from here to…L?"

"No, that's the other part of the job. You may be called upon to…um, escort them. In or out. Or both. "

"This sounds more fun by the moment, sir. You don't mean that I'll be going along with…"

"Oh, no." Blake waved his hands in emphasis. "No, no. You will escort them aerially, but not as a team member, so to speak."

"Okay, I think I have the big picture. When do I volunteer for this?"

"You just did. I've already told you more than I could unless you were already on board. So you are, by default."
134

"Oh good. Never let it be said that I didn't have a choice."

"Good boy. Now, since that was the adumbrated version, you'll be formally briefed by a Ranger, and then you can start immediately."

"You mean the usual kind of immediately; where by the time I hear about it, I'm already late for takeoff?"

"Not this time. Your first mission isn't until tomorrow."

"Wonders never cease. When is this briefing?"

He grinned. "You're already late. Inside here." Blake ushered him onto a concrete stairway that led down below ground – to a bunker where Rusty had never been before. A waist-high pile of sandbags several yards square was festooned with a veritable porcupine of antenna masts – the only visible clues that anything unusual was there at all.

At the bottom of the stairs, Blake pushed a doorbell button three quick times: short, long, short.

"R in Morse? For Rusty, or for reluctant?"

"For Ranger, silly boy."

The door opened, and Blake took Rusty's elbow and guided him quickly inside – almost roughly. The door slammed shut again, and a lock clicked. By the time Rusty's eyes adjusted, he was able to see a short narrow corridor leading off to his left, and another open door in the wall directly ahead of him. He walked ahead through the second door.

"Have a seat, Lt Naille." It was a tall man in an Army uniform, but without a nametag, rank or unit badges. He looked like he could run a mile in three minutes, rip phone books in half and kill you using only his fingernail clippings as weapons. Even his eyes were the color of gunmetal. "We're delighted to have you aboard."

135

"Uh huh," Rusty said warily. He sat in the room's only chair, a steel folding job that faced a blanket-covered chalkboard.

"As you've been told, or may have surmised, the mission of the Ranger patrols is to gather intelligence about enemy activity and movement. Some of those patrols may or may not, at times, work beyond the accepted and acknowledged limits of the war, as stated by our national leaders. Do you follow?"

"I get it. You do stuff old Tricky Dicky would rather not have bandied about."

The man almost smiled. "That understates it nicely. If I may do the same, what we are about to discuss may not be revealed to anyone whatsoever, under the penalty of pain."

"You mean the penalty of death?"

"Not immediately." He did not smile, even a little.

Neither did Rusty.

Most of what followed just mirrored or amplified what Blake had told him, except for the fact that many of the teams were composed of "mixed nationalities." But that shouldn't have surprised Rusty; it made sense to use people who may know the local language, could deal with tribes and such. The only surprise was the fact that something about all this *was* sensible.

Rusty was pre-flighting his plane for his first "black" mission the next day, when a jeep pulled up and a guy in the Army's two-piece, olive green flight suit clambered out. He was a fireplug of a man, short but very powerful looking, with the round, broken face of a boxer or a mobster thug. Tiny black eyes peered out of that face; under the lumpy, twisted nose was a mouth that looked like it should have been clamped around a stub of a cheap cigar. His flight suit had no nametag or other insignia.

"You Naille?" he said, already slipping into his parachute. His voice was a cigar-smoking, whiskey-guzzling growl.

136

"Uh huh. You?"

"Joe."

"You betcha. 'Joe.' Ok, Joe, I'll climb in and you climb in after me. Got it? This is called a plane. Should I spell that?" Rusty didn't know why he was acting like such a jerk, but the back-alley tough looks of this guy just seemed to set him off.

"No."

They strapped in without another word, and Rusty started the engines, did the checks, taxied and got the rockets armed as if he'd been solo: wordlessly. But after they got airborne, he turned a bit to the man and said, "Look, I'm sorry. I was a jerk back there. Maybe this is just too weird for me. The mission, I mean. Uh, Joe."

Joe looked at him from the corner of his left eye. "Actually, you was a complete prick. But ..." He held out his hand.

Rusty stuck his into Joe's, and immediately regretted it. It felt as though he might see blood squirting out of his glove at any second. Then Joe released it. "Uh, that's fine. I didn't need that one, anyway. Much."

Joe bellowed a laugh. Bellow would be mild – he almost blasted the windows out.

Rusty smiled. Well, maybe Joe wasn't so bad.

They flew west, and west some more. Finally, Rusty said, "Um, I hate to say this, Joe, but I'm out of maps. I'm off the edge of my last one. I don't know what to do now."

Joe reached into the calf pocket of his flight suit and pulled out a sheaf of maps. He peeled off the outer one, and handed it to Rusty. "Here ya go. I got more."

"I just bet you do, Joe." He oriented himself on this one, noting that it was annotated in French. "This is a little old, isn't it? Is

137

it accurate?" They were still over Vietnam, but just barely, and the border here was indistinct at best.

"Enough. Orbit here. Big turns."

"Okey doke, Joe. Whatever you say. You boss, me taxi driver."

Joe reached over and squeezed Rusty's bicep. He grunted, unimpressed, then rasped, "Look. You ain't no Tarzan, and I ain't no chimp. Got it?"

"You're no Demosthenes, either."

"Demosthenes, dat Greek guy who became an orator by shoutin' against the sea with his mouth full of pebbles?" Joe asked.

Rusty almost fell out of the plane. "Okay, now this is beyond weird. You know who Demosthenes is?

"Was, Naille. Been dead a while. Yeah. You taxi drivers ain't the only ones who learned anyting. Maybe you tink I talk funny, but even I can read."

"Where'd you read about Demosthenes?"

Joe shrugged. "A book. 'Parallel Lives,' by that other guy."

"Plutarch. You've read Plutarch."

Joe shrugged again. "Yeah. Wanna make sumthin of it?"

Rusty shook his head, stunned to silence. A little while later, he turned to Joe again and asked, a bit slyly, "So…why the rocks?"

"He stuttered."

"Son of a bitch." He stuck out his hand again, but then blanched and snatched it back just in time.

Joe bellowed another laugh, and they were friends.

They'd made three huge circles when Rusty thought he heard a faint scratching in his headphones. Puzzled for a second, he said, "Hey Joe, do you…"

"SHHH! It's dem." Joe huddled down, eyes scrunched tight, then shot them open and reached for his own grease pencil. He wrote a series of numbers on his window: 11, 23, 64, 7, 25, 88, 51, 3, 18. Rusty heard him reply in an equally faint rasp, "Six, twenny-two, niner, forty-tree." When no reply came for several minutes, he turned to Rusty, "It's code."

"I'll be damned. You're sure it's not a football play?"

"Yeah, okay…smart ass. Nah. Can't risk words, mostly. Da bad guys got radios too, ya know."

"Uh huh. So now what?"

"Orbit a while longer. In case. Den we're done."

"That's it? That's all this cloak and dagger stuff amounts to?"

"On good days, yeah. Not all good days, tho."

"Yeah, I can imagine that. Hairy, huh?

"Like dat chimp."

Rusty grinned. "Joe, you're all right."

"You too, Naille. Guess da guys was wrong." He punched Rusty on the arm, lightly. It would only be green and purple for a few days.

Back at Emerald, Rusty went to see Blake, as instructed.

"How was it?"

"Mostly boring. My rider was interesting. A bit like a Neanderthal with a New Jersey Italian accent."

"Hmm, sounds…interesting. What'd you two talk about?"

"Greek orators." Rusty said, smirking.

"Well, if I'd wanted a smart-ass answer, I would've asked for it," Blake said.

Before Rusty could reply, the military field phone on Blake's desk gave its whirring buzz. Blake lifted the receiver out of the side compartment, identified himself and listened. Rusty saw Blake's face go white, then visibly sag. Blake dropped the headset back into the box.

"What is it?" Rusty asked.

"Palmer. He's overdue."

They radioed nearby bases and even emergency landing strips. No reports of a Baggy Zero Five landing anywhere. Five hours after Crazy Eddie took off, they started the steps to have him listed as missing. The O-2 only carries 4.5 hours of fuel.

Regular missions for the rest of the day were cancelled. Brian and Rusty took off to fly search patterns. The Army started running pink teams as well. Nothing. For two more days, they did nothing but fly search missions. Still nothing.

At breakfast on the third day, Major Whitworth asked Brian to pack up Eddie's personal effects.

"No, I'll do that," Rusty said. "I still owe Eddie something, and…" he couldn't finish, a lump rising in his throat.

"All right, Rusty. You can do that. Just lay everything out, though. I'll come by and we can make a detailed inventory of everything," Blake said.

"Why?" Brian asked.

"As Mortuary Affairs Officer, I have to certify the inventory of everything that gets shipped back to Eddie's family. So that when it arrives, they know that they have it all. That nothing went…missing."

"Or stolen, you mean? By us?" Rusty flushed with anger.

"No, no. Not by you. No inference intended, Rusty. Never. But packages like that pass through many hands between here and there, and…"

"Oh. Oh, well. I see. Yes, that makes sense. Okay. I'll go lay it all out."

Rusty went through Eddie's locker, neatly piling everything he found. He held some items longer than others. Eddie's camera – there was half a roll of undeveloped film in it, Rusty noted; a new, boxed watch. Most poignant of all was a small album of family pictures that Rusty had never seen before. Nor could he recall Eddie ever looking at it. How private a guy he really was, marveled Rusty.

The word 'was' brought sudden tears to Rusty's eyes. He sat on the floor suddenly, weeping unabashedly. Brian sat on Rusty's bunk and didn't say a word. After a few minutes, Rusty wiped his face on his sleeve and went back to work, but he still snuffled a bit.

Before long, Blake came into the hooch. "Ah good. You've about finished. All right now; I'll start a list and you can sort this into two piles. One will be personal items and the other issued items. The issue stuff will stay, and his personals, along with a signed and witnessed list – that'll be you two and I – will go with it. A separate copy of that list will go to his files."

They did. When they got to a package of condoms and a well-thumbed issue of Playboy magazine, Blake shook his head. "Leave those out. This package is going to his mother, after all." When it was done, Eddie's effects only partially filled a duffel bag. "There's a foot locker in the jeep Brian. Will you fetch it? Meanwhile, I'll date and sign the list, then both of you can witness it."

"That's it?" Rusty asked dolefully. "That's all there is to losing a guy like Eddie?"

"No. Certainly not. But a lot of it happens out of our sight. The International Red Cross gets involved, Air Force Personnel Office of course, even the UN."

"The UN?"

"Yeah, Brian. In case Eddie has been captured. The Prisoners of War Council, or whatever it's called, starts an official inquiry."

"With North Vietnam? Fat chance that'll help. Fat chance that the NVA would keep a FAC alive, for that matter. They hate us. It'd be a quick bullet, most likely."

"They might, though. For the bounty."

"Bounty? What bounty?" Rusty blurted.

"Didn't you know? There's a ten thousand dollar bounty for the capture of any FAC. In gold. That's like a million bucks to your average VC – maybe more than a million," Blake said.

"I'd pay that right now," Rusty said, snuffling again. "It'd be worth it to have him back."

"Yeah, I'd double it," Brian said. "Cripes, now you got me doing it." He wiped his own eyes.

They closed and tied the duffel bag, placed it into the footlocker and locked that. Blake put the key into a brown paper envelope, sealed and initialed that. He turned, solemnly shook hands with Brian and Rusty; then drove off in the jeep, footlocker jouncing in the back seat.

"I'm glad I don't have to be there when the chaplain pulls up in front of Eddie's house," Brian said.

"Yeah, that has to be the world's worst job. But whoever it is probably didn't know Eddie like we did."

"What do you think happened?" Brian handed a beer to Rusty.

"Who knows? He loved to fly down those rivers. Maybe he went down low to see something and snagged a wingtip or something. The way those rivers are roaring now, there wouldn't be a trace of anything left. Even if there were, it'd be miles downstream from where he hit. Maybe even out in the South China Sea by now."

"You don't think…" Brian turned to look east.

"No, not a chance. Hell, we don't even wear flotation vests, much less a raft. Those weeks of sea survival training we all took were just a feel good exercise. Besides, he'd have had to make it all the way down through those boulder-filled rapids first. No."

"No, I guess not. Even if he did land in a river. Chances are he didn't. If he hit in that triple-canopy jungle, there wouldn't even be a trace of the wreckage to see from above. It'd close up again just like water."

"Uh huh. You think he took a hit?" Rusty asked.

"That's most likely, if you ask me. The Golden BB."

"The one with his name on it? You believe in that? Of all the ten bazillion bullets the VC fire at us, that one of them is fated to get us?"

"I'm less metaphysical than that, Rusty. But if one of them does hit you, it certainly did have your name on it."

"That's true enough. What'd Eddie tell me the other day: that all this is bass-ackwards? He was right. If it gets you, it had your name, whether the engraving came first or later."

"Amen to that."

"And to Eddie." The elegiac tunk of beer cans in the growing dusk wasn't crystal, but then neither had been Eddie Palmer.

CHAPTER NINE

"I tink mebbe we find sumptin' today, Naille," Joe said as they trundled west.

"How so, Joe?"

"Dose numbers we got de other day meant dat de team is watchin' bad guys. Lotsa bad guys."

"Really? Are we going to get involved with their little game? Give them something else to watch, perhaps?"

Joe grinned. "Just maybe."

"I just might enjoy that."

Joe handed him a map. "See dis speckled space?"

"Yeah, those green spots mean it's a plantation. Rubber or banana, usually."

"Dis one's rubber. Michelin Tires: da fucking Frenchies. But it's owned by da local bigwig, da provincial chief. He built dat temple right in de middle."

"Why did he do that, Joe?" Rusty asked rhetorically, anticipating the answer.

"'Cause it ain't legal to bomb any religious structures. And he knows dat. So his trees stay fat, and so does his Swiss bank account."

"And how does this plantation interest us, Joe?"

"It is interestin' when a couple towsan NVA use da place for an R&R site."

"Ah. Yes, that would make it very interesting. But what can we do about it?"

Joe flashed a lopsided grin, and told Rusty the plan.

When he'd finished, Rusty's eyebrows had lifted way up inside his helmet. "You think we can get away with that? My wings might be on the line if we get caught."

"You'll be fine. Trust me. Dis ain't just my brain bomb. Capiche?"

"I think I do, Joe. But it would be wiser if I didn't speculate?"

"See, I tole dose guys you was smart. You do it jus da way I said, we both be fine."

"I'm in."

"You already was."

"Uh huh. Seems like I keep hearing that." He laughed.

Joe shrugged his shoulders – no easy task when you have no neck - and laughed, too.

A few minutes later, Joe stabbed a sausage of a finger onto the map and then out the window. "Dat's it. See da temple?" Rusty nodded. "Now look wit da glasses."

Rusty focused the binoculars, and saw dozens, no…hundreds of men in light green uniforms and pith helmets, strolling about, cooking, even lounging on the stone steps of the small temple located in the exact center of a rubber plantation. The square plantation stretched a kilometer on each side, and no matter where Rusty looked, he could see NVA regular soldiers as thick as ants.

"Damn, Joe, that's the most enemy soldiers I've ever seen. Hell, LZ Emerald doesn't have that many of our own soldiers. How many are there?"

"We tink about five grand. The team can't get a good count, they's so many."

146

"I'm not surprised. Where is the team, anyway? Just so I know when it all starts."

"See dat little hill about a click to da east? Right on top. Been dere for a week. No fires, no hot chow. Only one asleep at a time. Dey don't even talk."

"No talking? How do they communicate?"

"Hand signals, little notes, little hand clickers, dat's all."

"What happens if one of them snores?" Rusty joked.

Joe drew his thumb across his throat. He wasn't smiling.

"And after all this?"

"Dey move off real quiet, and den we go get 'em. If dey get away."

No shit, Rusty thought. He thought the Loach guys' job was like sticking a hand into a hornet nest. These guys were sticking their dicks into one.

"Almost time, Joe. The fighters will be checking in any…"

"Baggy Zero Four, Cobalt Zero Six with you, flight of two F-4s." He gave their position and altitude.

Rusty acknowledged them, read the mission number of the pre-planned strike that Joe had given him, asked for their ordnance load and fuel status.

"Baggy, Cobalt six and wing are wall-to-wall CBU, as requested. Twenty minutes play time."

Without transmitting, Rusty turned to Joe, "Are the fighters in on this?"

"No. Da fewer da better. Just do like I said."

"Okay. Here goes." He flipped the selector back to transmit. "Cobalt Six, your target is a suspected troop encampment. Coordinates are…" he read the series of numbers on the slip of paper that Joe held out. "There are no friendlies in the area." Rusty held up his fingers, crossed. "Target area has a special restriction. There is a religious structure about two kilometers from the target coordinates. Under no circumstances are you to hit within one kilometer of the religious structure. Acknowledge."

"Roger, Baggy. Cobalt Six acknowledges. No drops within one click of the religious structure. Two?" "Two acknowledges." "Okay Baggy, have you in sight. Ready for your mark."

"Stand by for a mark, Cobalt. Oh, no need for a wheel. This one's just a sky puke, I think. Just make one pass, joined up. Copy?"

"Uh, roger that, Baggy. One pass, haul ass, holding hands. Standing by."

Rusty took one more look through the binoculars. Now that he was much closer, he could see individual NVA soldiers looking up and pointing at him from their inviolate Buddhist sanctuary. On the very steps of the pure white temple, one of them had his pants down. He was mooning Rusty.

"All right, asshole," Rusty said, stuffing the binoculars away. He rolled in, flipped his switches and aimed more closely than he ever had. WHOOSH! The white phosphorous warhead burst – right on the steps of the temple. "Cobalt flight, do *not* hit the religious structure. Hit my smoke, *do you copy*?" Everything - this mission, his career, even his life outside a prison - depended on what Rusty heard next.

"Uh…" In the pause, Rusty's heart stopped. Oh God, let them understand…

"Uh, roger that, Baggy. We do. We copy big time. Lead's in hot." "Two's in hot."

"Cobalt flight, you are cleared hot." He released the mic button, stabbed his right fist in the air and yelled, "This one's yours, Eddie."

The big green jets, almost wingtip to wingtip, plunged down out of the sky in a shallow dive. A thousand feet over the edge of the plantation, each one simultaneously released eight long white canisters. All sixteen immediately split open, spewing thousands of bomblets into the hot sticky air.

On the ground, the NVA froze. Some ran, some ducked, some just stared in paralyzed disbelief, idiotic grins flashing to big-eyed terror. All to no avail. The plantation suddenly blazed like a 1,000-foot wide flashbulb. Billions of white-hot metal fragments buzz sawed through every living thing.

The jets pulled up into a turning climb just as Rusty heard that awful electrical buzz from thousands of not quite simultaneous blasts. Above the plantation lay a thin grey sheet of smoke that dissipated in moments. When he looked through the binoculars again, Rusty saw the same rubber trees, the same white stone temple, all apparently untouched and unchanged from the way they were minutes ago. There were no bomb craters, no fires. And not one living enemy soldier. Gore, pools of blood, whole bodies and shredded bodies, arms, legs, heads and more lay everywhere. With practically no evidence of how it all happened. Stomach suddenly churning, he tore his eyes from the carnage.

As soon as he got his heart and breathing back under control, Rusty keyed the mic again, "Uh, Cobalt Zero Six. BDA follows: One minute on target. 100% of bombs on specified target coordinates, no duds. Target area too obscured by thick jungle to provide damage assessment. Looks like just another monkey bust. Sorry."

"We copy, Baggy. Good bombs on the coordinates, no further assessment. We understand. Call us again. Any time."

Rusty turned to Joe, "You think it worked?"

Joe just grinned. "You did good. It worked. If dat scumbag plantation owner bitches about his trees, and dey listen to da radio tapes, what dey hear? Dat you hit a spot two clicks from here, a spot with just jungle. Da fighters agreed wit dat. On tape."

"How about the fighters?"

"You heard 'em. Dey understand, Naille. Hell, dey loved it. Call us anytime, dey said. No, dey got it. Hell, dey had to see, and dey dropped didn't dey?"

"Yeah. Yeah, they did! They *did* get it! Goddamn, we might get away with this. You think I said everything all right? Really?"

"Ain't no rocks in yore mouth." He playfully punched Rusty in the arm again.

It would heal.

Two days later, Rusty and Joe escorted a force of helicopters, two unarmed Huey "slicks" and two fierce Cobra gunships, out west. The team had crept, crawled and slunk their way five kilometers from the plantation, and was huddled down next to a grassy clearing. They were ready to "exfil," the military opposite of infiltrate. In short, they were ready to go home – if anyone could consider LZ Emerald home.

"Don't mess around wit dis," Joe said. As soon as dey figger out what's goin' down, da bad guys'll be on dis like stink on shit."

"I figured that out myself, bud. So we do this just like we briefed: I get you nearby, you get the tem up on voice radio and authenticate they are who we hope they are, then they pop smoke. The slicks plop down, the team jumps on board, and we scoot. Right?"

"Dat's da plan. Only one ting."

"What's that?"

"Da plan is da first to die when da shootin' starts."

"So be ready to improvise."

"Yeah. Dat's where we see if you any good. Or if you kill off my frens." Once again, he wasn't smiling.

Rusty blew out a long breath. "We'll see."

"Fly dat way, not too near da clearing." He stabbed his finger from the map to the ground. "It's right dere."

"I know that, Joe. I can read maps like you read books. Really." Rusty said, confidently.

"Okay. But dese are my buds, ya know?"

"I know, Joe. We'll get 'em home. Promise."

"I ain't like dis one is routine. We really pissed dose bad guys off. Dey gotta know how dat happened. Hell, just us being here with all dese whirlybirds tells 'em dere's a team here." Joe almost squirmed with anxiety.

"I know, Joe, I do. I personally guarantee this will work out fine." Rusty was amazed and touched by the soft center in this hulk of a man. Heck, he's a barbed wire Twinkie, thought Rusty, with a private giggle.

"Badger, this is Rabbit." The voice came through, hoarsely whispered.

"Go ahead, Rabbit," Joe whispered back.

"White Sox. Converse. Tampax."

"Ex Lax" said Joe, grinning.

Rusty turned to him, brows knitted.

"Dey said 'Dis the last place dey gonna run, period' and I says 'No shit'," Joe said. "Dat's dem." Then he transmitted again, "Do it."

Rusty looked down, and saw a plume of bright purple smoke grow from one corner of the clearing he'd been watching. At almost the same moment, a plume of yellow smoke rose from a different clearing a few hundred yards away.

Joe looked down, his face suddenly strained "Oh shit." He keyed his mike. "Two smokes, Rabbit. Two smokes. Concord?"

"Chardonnay, Badger. Chardonnay!"

"They're the yellow one, Naille. The other one's da bad guys. This is gonna be shitty."

"Yeah. Hang on." Rusty slammed the throttles forward, rolling and shoving the nose down. As he did, he changed the radio selector. "Cobra, Cobra, hit purple. Hit purple! Honeybee, watch me!" He dove as fast as the O-2 would go, aiming right at the clearing with the yellow smoke. Pulling back hard on the yoke, he zoomed right over the middle of the clearing, calling, "BINGO, BINGO, BINGO!" over the radio. Augering down from altitude, the two Huey slicks set up their landing approach to the clearing where Rusty had confirmed the team was. He looked back over his shoulder and saw twinkling white muzzle flashes and tracers from everywhere on the ground. Oh shit.

The first Huey got almost to a hover before it seemed to stumble in midair. It jerked and jittered sideways, then struggled to claw its way back upwards, trailing a thin skein of smoke. In surreal silence, it rose to a few hundred feet but then abruptly pitched over, rolling upside down and arrowing straight into the jungle. A plume of black smoke spurted upward.

"Honeybee Two is in." The second slick came to the clearing from a different direction, but aborted his pass before he even got near to a hover. "Heavy fire, Baggy. Aborting." While he made that short transmission, Rusty heard at least four bullet strikes over the pilot's microphone.

"Tell the team to run, Joe, this is no good. We'll never get a chopper in there alive."

Joe nodded and mashed his mic button. "Run, Rabbit, run."

"Dodge" was the reply.

"They'll move west," Joe explained.

"Back towards the plantation?" Rusty questioned.

"Might be da last place dey expect," Joe said.

Me too, thought Rusty. And it's over two miles away, too. Could they run that far through NVA-infested jungle? If they got there, then what? We have one helo shot up, one gone –four lives- and the Cobras must be running short of weapons, or soon would be. No choice. He spun the radio selector.

"This is Baggy Zero Four on Guard. Prairie Fire, Prairie Fire, Prairie Fire."

It was like yelling "Fire" in a packed theater. Prairie Fire was the code phrase that told the whole world a Special Operations team was in deep shit. It was a higher distress call than Mayday, and even more imperative than an aircrew rescue. And, he realized, because it was happening so close to his plantation strike – his highly illegal Buddhist temple strike – he'd likely be headed for Leavenworth after he landed. If he landed…

In the millisecond those thoughts flashed through his brain, he heard "Baggy Zero Four this is Crown on Guard. Copy Prairie Fire?"

"Affirmative, Crown. I declare Prairie Fire.

"Authenticate."

He thumbed through the Top Secret folder he carried only on these Special Ops missions until he found the code for today. "Tonto Six, Mike Five Eight."

"Stand by." Five seconds drug by. "Baggy Zero Four, Crown authenticates. Prairie Fire is active. Break. All aircraft, this is Crown on Guard. Stand by for Prairie Fire support. Report on 255 point one."

A whirlwind of fighters began checking in with Crown, all eager to help in a hot firefight with US lives at risk. Through the cacophony, Rusty heard "Badger....Rabbit...Come...in." The voice panted between rasps of breath. They were running – hard.

Joe stabbed his mic switch, "Gotcha, Rabbit. Go ahead."

"New...LZ...panel."

Rusty turned to the west, staring intently at every tiny clearing, every hole in the trees. Then he saw it: a strip of bright orange being rolled out on the ground. The clearing was barely a hundred meters across, but it was big enough for a single Huey to get in. "I see it!" Rusty said to Joe, "There!"

"Gotcha again, Rabbit. Sit tight"

"Hurry...they're...coming."

Rusty mashed his own mic, "Honeybee, say your status."

"Baggy, Honeybee Two is able. Two wounds, nothing bad. We'll try."

"Okay, good. I'll mark and you get in as quick as you can. Copy?"

"I see you, Baggy. Go ahead."

Rusty rolled in. He had intended to make a zooming pass and yell bingo when he passed over the clearing, but as he lined up on it, he saw a line of NVA soldiers explode out of the edge, running hard for where the team now hid. The team would be dead in seconds. Without looking, Rusty reached out and armed both rocket pods. He mashed his trigger not once but seven times as his sight tracked across
154

the center of the clearing. All fourteen smoke rockets flashed out in pairs, and burst into a veritable wall of incandescent white phosphorous and blinding white smoke. If it blinded the NVA long enough, maybe the team could run again.

"I sure see that, Baggy. Honeybee's going in….Taking fire now. Going in."

Joe turned to Rusty, fear in his eyes, "Whatcha gonna do now? Those are my guys down dere. You promised!"

"We have to buy that chopper 30 seconds of time, Joe. There's only one thing left to do. I'm gonna give those bastards a target they hate even worse than Rangers."

"What?"

"A FAC."

Rusty corkscrewed the plane back down again, but instead of mashing the throttles to the wall, he pulled them to idle. He leveled off only a hundred feet over the trees and slowed almost to a stall. Then he flew right over the NVA, as big, slow and hated a target as they'd ever seen – right in front of their noses.

Red and green tracers filled the sky around Rusty. He stared straight ahead, clenching his teeth and waiting for the bullets to rip into his body. PANK...PAPANK. One hit, and then two, and then PANKPAPANK...PINK..BANG...PAPANKPANK...PANK...PINK. In the midst of it, his canopy and side window shattered into a stinging hail of Plexiglas shards. He heard Joe grunt once with pain. Through half-closed eyes, Rusty saw the edge of the clearing pass almost leisurely under him. He firewalled the throttles again, hoping he still had engines at all. They both roared to life, and he started a climb. Looking left, he saw the Huey lifting off. He was about to transmit again when a cloud of grey smoke poured out from under his instrument panel, and he heard a sizzle of electrical sparks. The smoke burned his eyes, but he found the master battery and generator switches, slapping them all off. The sizzling stopped, and the choking smoke soon swirled out of the destroyed windows.

Had the team somehow gotten aboard the Huey? Knowing the answer was suddenly the most important thing in Rusty's mind. He flew on instinct. He forgot Joe. But he had to know. He banked and joined up with the Huey, passing it on the chopper's right. As he went by, he looked through the large cabin door and saw…a heap of bodies on the cabin floor, holding on for dear life. The one on top faced Rusty, though, and Rusty saw a mud-grimed, camouflaged, red-eyed…shit-eating grin.

Radios gone, intercom gone, instruments gone, windscreen gone, Rusty took stock. He looked out. Gas streamed from jagged holes in his wings. He looked at Joe and saw he was inexplicably grinning. Then he noticed the blood. A pool of it sloshed on the floor under Joe's seat.

Rusty leaned close to Joe and shouted, "You hit? You all right?"

Still grinning, Joe lifted his right boot and pointed. Half the boot's toe – and some of Joe's – were missing. Blood pumped out, but not in a huge stream. He'd not bleed to death.

Suddenly, Rusty had a sudden, overwhelming urge to check his own body. He ran his gloved hand over his belly and behind his back, looked at his legs and wiped his face. No blood. He let out a rush of breath he didn't know he'd been holding.

The wind in his face stung and made his eyes water, but he stayed in loose formation with the Honeybee as it flailed its way back to LZ Emerald. The two Cobras wove a protective pattern over them both, even though they had nothing left to fire. After a bit, the pile of bodies in the Huey untangled as the team found seats and seat belts. Joe leaned across Rusty and tried to count heads. When somebody on the Huey saw his round face, he jabbed at another team member and pointed. That man grinned back and gave Joe a big upraised thumb. Joe pounded Rusty's thigh with his huge hand.

It would heal.

Somehow, the landing gear worked, although the electrically driven flaps stayed up, and the landing was hard. Still dripping gas, Rusty shut the engines down at the end of the runway instead of attempting to taxi. Going up in a fireball after all they'd survived wouldn't be cool at all. Jeeps, fire trucks and an ambulance roared up to the plane. They got Joe out onto a stretcher, but he was sitting up and laughing when they slid it into the ambulance. "Hey, Naille! Tanks!" Rusty heard him bellow as they shut the doors.

Rusty wasted no more time in getting clear of the plane's hot engines and leaking fuel either. It could go up at any second. Whitworth was in one of the jeeps, and Rusty climbed in with him. Not until then did he remember: Crown!

"Oh shit! I declared a Prairie Fire emergency out there! What happened?"

"Oh, the Cobra pilots cancelled that. They talked to the Honeybee after you lost your radios, of course. When they knew the team was safe, they cancelled it. You had about a dozen sets of fighters headed your way, Naille. Now all of 'em are pissed because they couldn't get in on a Prairie Fire."

"Well, there's one FAC who's just fucking delighted to have gotten *out* of one." Then the other, darker thought occurred to him, "Uh, what about that? I mean, so near to that plantation and all?"

"That's Blake's realm, Rusty. Officially, I don't know anything about it. Nothing at all. But…"

Oh shit, here it comes, Rusty thought. Goodbye wings, hello Mister Handcuffs.

"But, I think what you might hear about that is…'What plantation?'"

CHAPTER TEN

Hours later, after Rusty had been debriefed by no fewer than four separate Special Operations guys – all in plain, insignia-free uniforms – he was allowed to go back to his hooch. Blake and Whitworth were waiting for him there with Brian. "You guys want the good news or the bad news?" Whitworth asked.

"Oh no, I knew it," said Brian. "That's why you only wanted to chit chat until Rusty got back, wasn't it?"

"Afraid so, Bigelow. So…which is it?"

"Bad news first, I guess," Rusty said. Brian nodded.

"Okay, here it is. LZ Emerald is closing. Is already closed, in fact. Operations are suspended effective immediately. We are no longer an active FAC operation."

"The Baggies are bagged?" Brian asked.

"Yeah, that sums it up pretty well. Went out with a helluva bang, but gone." He nodded to Rusty.

"Whoo. Man, I'm having a hard time coming to grips with all this at once. Too much happened to me today," Rusty said.

"I know. That's why we brought this." He nodded to Blake, who Blake unveiled another bottle of champagne. "You need a drink. Hell, we all need a drink."

Blake poured the bubbly stuff into four crystal wine glasses.

Whitworth looked at the glasses, one eyebrow raised. "Stolen from the Colonel's mess?" Blake grinned slyly. "Excellent!" Whitworth crowed. "So then…here's to Baggy FACs, past and present. To you, Josh, to you Brian, to you, Rusty…and to you, Eddie." He raised his glass toward the sky. "A chapter well closed."

"Hear, hear," they intoned, solemnly.

As Blake poured a second round, Brian piped up, "Hey! What's the good news?"

"Oh, right. Well, I'll start with you, Brian. You're going home. DEROS. You're going to be a T-37 instructor at Vance."

"YEE HAW! Oh man! That's great! When?"

"A few more days. I'll fly you down to Cam Rahn myself," Whitworth said.

"I told you, Brian. An instructor! You'll be a great one, bud," Rusty said, slapping Brian on the back.

"Rusty? That brings us to you. You have distinguished yourself here. I've recommended that you be upgraded to the OV-10 and assigned to one of the most elite FAC units. You deserve it."

"Wow. I don't know what to say."

"No need to say anything, Rusty," Blake chimed in. "I concurred on that recommendation – and one other. There's a Silver Star in the pipeline for you. The Special Ops guys are writing it up as we speak, and what they ask for, they get. Congratulations."

"A Silver Star? For Valor? I'm speechless. No, I'm speechlesser."

"Well, that'll be a first," Blake joked.

"Hey, what about you two?" Brian said.

"Oh, nothing as glamorous, I assure you. We're both going to the Air War College. Josh will be attending, and I've been picked to be on the faculty. Undeserved on my part."

"Bull," Blake said.

"Another toast! To choice assignments one and all!" Brian beamed.

They finished the bottle, and in its effusive aftermath, Rusty suddenly said, "Hey, how is Joe?"

Brian looked puzzled. "Joe? Who's Joe?"

"Oh, um, just a guy that Rusty flew with." Blake said.

"Ahh, a spook. I get it."

"Never mind." Turning to Rusty, he said, "He's fine. He'll have a limp for life, but that'll just add to his character, don't you think?"

"It couldn't help but enhance his image," Rusty laughed. "But I'm glad he's fine."

"So are the…others. All of them. Fine *and* glad."

Except for the four guys in Honeybee One, Rusty thought to himself. They hadn't a chance. Then he brightened. "Oh, that's great. I'm really relieved for them all."

When Whitworth and Blake had gone, Brian said, "That was nice. I couldn't believe Whitworth could limber up like that. Did you notice he used our first names? I've never heard him address anyone by his first name before."

"Yeah, and did you catch Blake's first name? Josh? Joshua do you think?"

"Must be. Sounds Jewish."

"Very. But what about the Blake part? That sure doesn't. That's English, isn't it? Like the writer?"

"I guess," said Brian. "Writers are over my thought horizon, mostly. But our Blake once told me that his grandparents were of
160

mixed faith. His grandfather was a Blake and his grandmother was a Rosenberg or Rosenblatt. Something with a 'Rosen' in it anyway."

"Ah, that makes sense. Jews are maternal. Your mother is Jewish, and that makes you Jewish. If your Dad is and your Mom isn't, then you aren't, unless you profess to it. Or I think that's the way it goes," Rusty said. "So he's Jewish from his grossmutter, and a Blake from his grossfadder."

"His who?"

"Grandparents. In Yiddish."

"I'll be damned," said Brian as he snapped out the lights.

The next few days were hectic, but in a completely different way than they were used to. There were no flying missions scheduled, for one thing. Blake had posted a blank flight schedule before breakfast the first day, and when Rusty commented about it, Blake said, "We can't take any chances with our only remaining airplane. Brian's got his DEROS, so he is off the sheet, and we certainly can't let you fly it, Rusty. You have a rather disconcerting habit of having holes installed in them."

Rusty laughed, but then asked. "I forgot to even look at that plane the other day. How bad was it?"

"Well, it's a good thing you were in the old plane and not the new one. It's a writeoff. We think the bullet that took off Joe's toe is the one that hit the underside of the instrument panel. It hit a major power supply bus and fried the electrical system. It's melted. Radios are dead, almost all the instruments are dead. And that's just the electricals. You took at least twenty hits, we think. Both wings and the tail are sieves, the right outboard fuel tank and both the left tanks had holes – you were lucky you made it back: almost no fuel dripped out after you shut down. A few quarts left, maybe. The hinge on the left wing flap is gone, the rear engine took two hits but kept running somehow with almost no oil left at all. And of course the windscreen and left window were blown out. I could go on…"

"Don't bother. I don't want to know."

"Then you don't want this?" He dropped a banana-shaped, scarred chunk of copper and lead into Rusty's hand."

"What is it?"

'That, my boy, is a spent bullet from an AK-47 assault rifle. It apparently came up through the floor and then through the single plate of Kevlar armor that's mounted under the left seat. The only armor in the O-2."

"And you found it…"

"Inside the left seat cushion. Just about where your…" He glanced down at Rusty's crotch.

"PHEW! Oh boy, I want to sit down." Then he laughed, "Hell, I'm just glad I *can* sit down!"

"Or get…up," Blake said, looking again at Rusty's crotch and winking.

"Maybe my life really is charmed," Rusty said after they'd both chuckled.

"That's what I told you once, but don't count on it. This is still Vietnam, and you can buy the farm at any time. There is such a thing as a bolt from the blue. But you should know that, too, lightning boy. Have you really been hit twice? You claimed that on your first day here."

"Yeah, I really was. Indirectly both times, but I did have all the hair on my right arm burned off the first time. It left me shaking and quivering for hours. My muscles just wouldn't stop twitching."

"I'm not surprised. Just hearing it makes me twitch."

Rusty thought about lightning, and Golden BBs, and as they walked from the TOC to the FAC Shack, Rusty cast a surreptitious

162

glance at the sky. Thunder rumbled in the distance, and Rusty shivered once.

The Army went about closing LZ Emerald in the way the Army does everything – with destructive zeal. Bulldozers rumbled down rows of troop tents, crushing bunks, lockers, wooden floors, canvas tents and sandbag walls into mounds of splinters and dirty rags.

Brian pulled up in front of the FAC hooch and called inside, "Hey Rusty! Let's go make noise!"

"Huh?"

The Army has tons of ammo left over, and they have no intention of hauling it out of here or letting Charley get it, so they're letting anybody shoot all they want before they blow it up. Let's go!"

Rusty jumped into the jeep and they drove to the southern edge of the camp. There, the barbed wire wall looked out over a wide cleared strip to the edge of the jungle. Stacked there were crates of small arms ammo, hand grenades, grenade launchers, and more. An Army sergeant pointed to a stack of rifles, both US and VC, and said. "Pick anything you like and have at it, sirs. Just keep all your shots that way," he pointed to the jungle, and do not fire towards the rice paddies over there," he pointed to the southeast.

Brian picked an M-16, but Rusty, conscious of the spent bullet he had in his front pants pocket, picked up an AK-47. With little-boy grins, they held the guns at their hips, looked out over the barbed wire, and started shooting. They shot at dirt clods. They shot at trees, and they shot at the splash of dirt from the other guy's last shot. They emptied magazine after magazine until the gun barrels were smoking hot, and then they switched to other guns. Rusty fired a grenade launcher, giggling at the ridiculous little "poonk" sound it made when it fired and lobbed its 40-millimeter grenade the 200 yards to the tree line. There, the projectile exploded with a satisfying bang much louder than the firing sound. They fired a "grease gun" .45-caliber machine pistol left over from WWII, and were amazed at how cheaply it had been made, but how utterly reliable it was for launching its massive pistol bullets downrange. They even lined up for a chance to fire the devastating .50-caliber Browning machine gun mounted to a tripod in the back of a jeep. That was incredible, but so loud that Rusty cringed with every shot.

Through it all, they laughed and grinned at each other like schoolboys. They ran from gun to gun and yelled as they flung empty ammo cans down the dirt wall. They even laughed when their fingers closed on hot rifle barrels. They shot guns until their faces were black with gun smoke, their hands were blistered and their ears rang incessantly. It was, in short, a hoot.

Rusty even got an invitation to fly one of the little Loach helicopters he had worked with on so many pink teams. He jumped at the chance, and even Blake approved, albeit grudgingly at first. But when he saw the glee in Rusty's eyes, he simply couldn't deny him this rare opportunity.

Rusty met with one of the young warrant officers who took on this most dangerous job. Craig was his name, and he got Rusty strapped into the observer's seat of the tiny egg-shaped craft. Luckily, both seats had working controls, and as soon as they got airborne, Craig said, "You want to try it?" Rusty snatched at the controls with both hands and both feet. Immediately, he discovered that the thing was incredibly light and fast in its response to even the tiniest control input. Just *think* and the craft would leap in some direction or other. Not always the one Rusty had thought about moving, he quickly discovered. In a helicopter, to do one thing, you have to simultaneously do about three other things, he soon discovered. But in just a few minutes, he was able to hold altitude, turn and dash in any direction he wanted to. It was like flying a magic carpet, he thought to himself, by mind control alone.

In a few minutes, Craig said. "Why don't you try a hover? I'll follow you on the controls so you can't make any major mistakes, but you'll be in control. Just lower the collective a tad and let it settle down. Drift to the center of that clear spot right there. When you get close to the ground, you'll find that ground effect cushions your descent and you'll almost be in a hover. Then just try to hold it still.

Remember, you don't want to actually move the stick or anything. Just tiny amounts of pressure will do."

Rusty did as he'd been instructed. The craft settled towards the ground slowly, and when they were only about five feet above it, it seemed as though they'd touched down on a pillow of some kind. "Okay, there's the ground effect. Now, just keep your eyes out front on a distant object and try to hold us perfectly still."

Rusty couldn't quite do that – it was like balancing a broom on one's nose while standing on a teeter-totter – but he managed to avoid touching the ground or shooting too far in any other direction.

"Hey, you're good. Cripes, it took me three weeks at primary training before I could hover even half that well. You sure you've never done this before?"

"Nope," said Rusty tersely, concentrating so hard he thought his eyes would burst out of his head, "Never."

"Jesus. Golden fucking hands," mumbled the man.

Rusty couldn't help smiling to himself at that – and promptly lost control of the chopper.

"Oops a daisy," said Craig, taking control and stabilizing the craft before it hit anything. "Okay, maybe you better quit while we're both ahead." With that, he zipped the little bird upwards and Rusty relinquished control. Craig now took pride in showing off his skill. He dropped the Loach into tiny holes in the trees, sometimes even clipping off leaves and small branches with the invisibly fast, humming rotors. At one point, he flew under them, dropping down into a green tunnel of overhanging limbs and hovering along underneath until he found another patch of sky to pop up through.

"Uh, that's really impressive, but what if we aren't alone down here, Craig? We don't have any Cobras covering us, you know."

"Oh yeah, that's right. Jeez, maybe I got carried away there. Okay, let's head back to the barn. Had enough?"

"To last me a lifetime, my friend. I know what I do, and I thought that was dangerous. But this? No thanks. I'll admit, though, this is an amazing little buggy. What I wouldn't give to have one of these afterwards."

"Me too. But I don't think a warrant officer is ever gonna earn enough to buy one. Even a used one. So I'm making the most of this while I still can."

"Yeah," agreed Rusty. "Can you believe Uncle Sugar pays us to fly things like this? Helicopters, jets, even that sky pig of an O-2. Life couldn't be better."

"Nope. Sure can't. No matter what happens after this, it's something I'll never forget as long as I live."

None of us will, Rusty thought to himself. None of us. Ever.

That evening, he and Brian sipped the last of the Carling Black Label while they packed. Rusty stood and looked at the empty top bunk where Eddie had slept. His eyes stayed dry this time, but his heart sank in his chest. They really would be leaving him behind.

"Don't forget these," Brian said, pointing to the new pictures of Mary Beth that she'd sent him. It jarred Rusty back to the present and happier things.

"No. No, I sure won't. Thanks." He folded the picture frames into a tee shirt and laid them carefully in the center of his duffel bag for safety. "Hey, listen. It's our last night in this dump. Tomorrow we move out and they'll bulldoze this place. I think one last Baggy FAC shower is in order."

"Hey, yeah. Good idea. You wanna stoke it up, or should I?"

"I'll take that honor," Rusty said. "I've had two more beers than you, and it's a job that requires extra lubrication."

Brian laughed at the nonsensical line, and Rusty stuffed a pack of matches into his shirt pocket. Outside, it was dark already, but Rusty felt his way up the rickety ladder. "Hey Brian, damn good thing we're leaving - this ladder is about shot."

"Yup," came the laconic answer.

Rusty checked that the garbage can was full of cold water. He jiggled the toilet valve and fresh water came in. Yup, working fine, he thought to himself. He cracked the fuel valve a touch and could smell the characteristic odor of high-octane aviation gas as it started to drip down the intake pipe. He got out the matches, but the first one didn't light. Damn things are wet, he mumbled. He tried again, but still no luck. The third one lit, and he leaned over to drop it into the pipe. WHOOMP!

For a split-second that seemed like ten, he watched in fascination as a boiling, writhing, doughnut of fire shot up the pipe and into his face. Involuntarily, his eyes clamped shut. With a shrill cry of pain and anguish, Rusty stumbled backwards, feeling for the ladder. His hand grasped it and he stepped down. But what he'd thought was the right ladder riser was the left, and his foot met nothing but air. Falling, he mindlessly stuck out his left arm to catch himself, and then he thudded to the ground. There was a clearly audible snap, and then – nothing.

He woke in a panic. Everything before him was blackness. He must have cried out and bolted up, because he felt a hand on his chest, pushing him back down gently but firmly. "Now sir, just take it easy. You're okay; it's just the bandages. Your eyes are fine. Don't panic. Your friends here can watch you now."

Then he heard Blake's voice. "That's right, Rusty. Be calm. I'm here. Trust me. It's all right."

He lay back, and when he was flat again, he became aware of a heavy weight across his chest. He tried to move his arm and was shocked by a jolt of piercing pain.

"Oh, don't try to move, Rusty. Just be calm, like I said. It's just a broken arm, and that's your cast. But don't try to move it, okay?" Blake went on, in the singsong voice people use with sick children.

"What…Oh, wait. I remember. The water heater. How'd I get…I mean…"

"You fell off the fucking roof, you dolt." It was Brian. "After you blew your eyebrows off. Geez, what a hockey puck."

Rusty couldn't help smiling. "It was the wet matches. It took three, and by then…"

"By then you had enough avgas in the bottom of that thing to fly an Oscar Deuce to Thailand," Blake finished. "Heck, you almost flew that far *without* an Oscar Deuce."

Rusty quickly became more lucid. "My arm? You said it's broken."

"Yeah. And as usual, you did a bang-up job. Damned near made me puke when I saw it." Brian said. "Ewwww."

"Huh?"

"Oh man, it looked like you had two wrists, and bones stuck out all over like from a bag of uncooked spaghetti. Gross."

"Blake here paints perhaps too graphic a picture." Rusty heard a thud and a stifled grunt. "But your arm is fine now. It will heal perfectly well, the doctors assure me, and without question you will be back in the cockpit in due course."

"Uh, okay. My eyes?"

"Oh, yes. No problem. You did indeed lose your eyebrows and eyelids; and there may be some slight discomfort, but again, the doctors say that there is no permanent damage to your eyes. There'll be tests when the bandages come off, as a matter of routine, but they say there's no reason to fear for your eyesight. At all, Rusty."

He felt Blake's hand squeezing his. Under the bandages, he could feel tears forming.

He croaked out, "Thanks. Uh, Mary Beth? Did anyone..."

"Yes, I've already sent her a message through the Red Cross. I got her address from the envelopes – I didn't read the letters – in your duffel. The Red Cross will say that you've had a non-combat injury and are recovering nicely. That's all. If you wish to be more detailed, you can tell her in person."

"In...what did you say?"

"In person. Well, in light of this," Rusty heard and felt Blake tapping the plaster cast that went from his left fingertips to his shoulder, "You're going home. Your tour is over. Too early, and a terrible waste of FAC talent, but that's the way it is."

"Going home? But what about my OV-10? What about..."

"On hold, I think would be the best way to break it to you, son. There's no way the United States Air Force will condone having you mope around here in the Vietnamese vacationland while unemployable in your chosen profession. So they've taken the disagreeable option of sending you home while you recuperate. You'll be back here soon enough. They haven't yet gotten their full pound of flesh from you, you know."

"Says the Merchant Shylock?" Rusty quipped.

"Now I know you're awake, Blake sighed loudly. "You've begun insulting my heritage again."

"Cripes, if you two are turning literary again, I'm leaving," Brian said. Rusty heard a chair scrape and footsteps.

Rusty whispered to Blake, "Is he gone? Man, he was sure odd. I never heard Brian talk like that before."

"I think he's one of those people who simply cannot stand the sight of blood or injury, Rusty. He was whiter than you were when I got to you both."

"Uh, fill me in. I don't remember anything after the heater backfired."

"Well, you apparently fell off of or missed the ladder altogether. Brian said he heard the heater go bang, and then a cry, and then a second or two later, a loud thud. He ran out and found you unconscious. He rolled you over, and that's when he saw your arm. He denies it, but there was a distinct smell of slightly used beer about the place when I got there."

"He peed his pants?"

"Worshipped BUUUdha. Bought a BUUUick in EUUURope. From RAAAlph. In short, he barfed his guts out. But don't tell him I said so," Blake winked mischievously, then realized Rusty still had eye patches on. "Anyway, the sight of you scared him. He ran up to our hooch yelling and banging on our door loud enough to wake the dead. I ran down while Frank called the hospital. They sent a litter down and carried you here. Oh, 'here' is the field hospital at Emerald, by the way. But you won't be here long."

"I want to know what that means, but first, how was my arm. Really. As bad as Brian described?"

Blake debated what to say, then shrugged to himself. "You deserve the truth. Yeah. I've never seen a worse break. Compound complex I think they call it. Both bones, just above the wrist, and the shattered ends of the bones were sticking out."

"Like Brian said? Uncooked spaghetti?"

"Couldn't have said it better myself. It was gruesome. But, let me now absolve the sin of telling you that by saying that the docs here worked their asses off getting everything aligned again and set. They worked on that arm for seven hours."

"Seven...what time is it now?"

"Now? Oh, it's mid morning. And that brings me to the rest of our discussion. There's a C-130 due in here in a couple of hours. You'll be on it. You'll go to Tan San Nhut, then onto a Freedom bird for medevac – probably tomorrow or the next day since you aren't critical. You'll be in the US in 48 hours or thereabouts."

Doctors came in and checked Rusty out before Rusty could ask any more questions of Blake, but he had quite a few for the doctors. Yes, they assured him, what Blake had said was undeniably true: He'd fly again, his arm would heal just fine, and he was scheduled for immediate but non-critical medevac. "You like milk?" the doctor asked as he was leaving.

"Uh, yeah. If it's real. Not the dried hog swill they serve here."

Rusty could almost feel the grin he got back. "Good. Then we'll put it on your chart: all the milk and ice cream you can get down. Medicinal. For the bones, you understand. Administered by genuine US blue-eyed, round eyed nurses. Suit you?"

Rusty could feel himself crying again under his eye patches. "Uh huh." He choked out.

During those few hours, Whitworth came in and said his goodbyes. He even hugged Rusty. Brian came back and managed an awkward but warm goodbye, and even the enlisted guys stopped in to wish him the best. None of the Army officers bothered. The medical staff fed him, bathed him and fitted him with a comfortable sling for his cast. The time flew by, and before he knew it, they got him onto a stretcher, carried him out and drove him down to the flightline. As he jounced along, Rusty wished he could get one last look at the FAC Shack. Oh well, it and that shower would lurk forever in his mind.

He felt himself being carried up the sloped rear ramp of the C-130 on a stretcher. They strapped him in, gently but firmly. Then he heard Blake's voice again.

"Rusty, I just wanted to say one final thing as a goodbye. I mean this from the bottom of my heart. I never met a better pilot than you, nor a better, more talented FAC. And that says something, because there is no, repeat *no*, more difficult or more demanding flying job in the world. How we find the young men to…but don't let me get started. I wanted to tell you: you were the best I ever saw, period. If they ever commission a statue to all FACS, they should use you as the model. Good luck. I'll be following your career, even if we never meet again."

There was a pause, and Rusty heard a sniff. Then, "Oh, one more thing. Here. It's from another guy who admired you a lot. Said the same thing about you that I just did, in fact. He said it's for you." Rusty felt a thick book being pressed into his right hand, but before he could say anything else, the flight engineer yelled to Blake to get off the plane if he was going. Rusty heard a muffled, choked-off "Bye," and then motors whined, the ramp clanged shut and the four big turboprop engines started, drowning out Rusty's sobs.

Over the Pacific Ocean, the big, comfortable medevac jet whispered along. Rusty, now riding in a regular seat, slurped down ice cream shake after shake, with ice-cold milk chasers. All of it real, rich and delicious beyond measure. He was relaxing in a dairy stupor when a nurse with exquisitely soft hands and a voice to match said, "Lt Naille? The doctor says that if you'd like, we can remove your eye patches now. If it's too bright or painful, we can put new ones on, but he'd like to take a peek at your eyes. Is that all right?"

"Oh yeah. I'm ready."

They gently removed the patches and swabbed the gunk and old medicine out of his eyes, then told him to open his lids. It was bright, and almost painful, but Rusty forced himself to keep them open, even if he had to squint. Things slowly came into focus, and the first thing he saw clearly was the nurse's face. She was a redhead, with emerald green, gold-flecked eyes, and Rusty would remember them much more fondly than his nose would remember that first awful whiff of Cam Rahn Bay air all those months ago. She wasn't Mary Beth, but she was an angelic vision, nonetheless.

She smiled at him and said, "Good. I'm very happy for you. You're one of the lucky ones." She patted his hand and moved on to other patients.

"I'm charmed," he said smiling at the secret joke.

Suddenly, Rusty remembered the book. He had assumed it was a Bible, from the pebbly feel of the worn leather covers, but he was curious to learn who had given it to him.

He fished it out of his small carry-on bag and turned it over.

On the cover, in faded gold leaf, it said, "Parallel Lives" and under that, "Plutarch." Inside the front cover, Rusty read the blocky, erratic scrawl, "None in your head, either." It was signed Vito Ragusa, but that name had a single line diagonally through it, and after that, "Joe."

Rusty turned the flyleaf. Inside that was stamped: "Property of the Boxwood Reformatory School Library"

He laughed until his eyes ran again, and the green-eyed nurse ran back to him, "Is something wrong?"

Rusty waved his right palm at her. "No. Something is finally right."

The End